MW00986119

Life of His Party

Broken Blue Gay Romance Series, Volume 3

DJ Monroe

Published by Pinwheel Books, 2019.

This is a work of fiction. Similarities to real people, places, or events are entirely coincidental.

LIFE OF HIS PARTY

First edition. June 12, 2019.

Copyright © 2019 DJ Monroe.

ISBN: 978-1073530588

Written by DJ Monroe.

Chapter 1

Richard leaned against the fender of the big, brand new pickup and folded his arms. It was a gorgeous blue-sky day in late February, and even though it was still cold spring was most definitely on its way. The equipment deal was done, and now he could relax for a few moments in the company of his guest.

The guest who was currently looking him up and down like he was a nicely marbled ribeye.

OK, so maybe relax was the wrong word, because Richard was pretty damned uncomfortable under Marshall Niven's steady blue-eyed gaze. The glint in his eyes only brightened when Richard cleared his throat and smiled.

"So...we can expect the new equipment by the end of next week?" Richard asked. He knew the answer, but he was trying to deflect Marshall's attention, which was hovering somewhere around Richard's belt buckle.

Richard shuffled his weight from one foot to the other. Marshall had never hidden his interest, because why would he? The guy was rich and arrogant and not ashamed of his playboy lifestyle at all. Not Richard's type. In fact, the opposite of Richard's type.

Of course, it had been a long time since Richard even had a type.

"Yep. It'll be on its way within a day or two. You might even get it earlier than that." Marshall grinned at him and took a step closer, his breath puffing a little in the chilly air. "We aim to please, you know."

It wasn't that Marshall was ugly or creepy. In fact, a few years ago Richard would have jumped at the chance to meet a guy like him. Not these days, though. Marshall was a well-known player, and Richard's life was so far beyond casual hook-ups that the idea was laughable. The tightness in his belly wasn't the good kind - it was more stress than pleasure.

"Well, if that's all, I guess I'll be getting back to work, then. The grind never ends, does it?" Richard winced at his own choice of words.

"Well, we can hope not."

OK, now Marshall *was* getting a little creepy.

"Do you ever get away from that pretty little lady of yours, Rich?" Marshall asked. He leaned against the fender, facing Richard. "Time to yourself?"

Richard stood and paced away, putting some air between them. "No, she'll keep me busy until she goes off to college, I suspect. Maybe longer than that."

How did he politely tell Marshall - one of their biggest partners at the Broken Blue - that he wasn't interested? Hell, he didn't know how to be interested. The last seven years had wiped out anything that resembled a dating life for Richard Gallagher, and he wouldn't know how to do the dating thing if it waltzed up to him and smacked his ass.

Luckily, Marshall didn't appear to be waiting for an answer. He patted the hood of the big truck, beeped the locks, and climbed into the driver's seat. He rolled down the window. "Well, you let me know if that ever changes, all right?"

"You bet. Take care, now." Relieved, Richard turned and sauntered back toward the main ranch house and his office in the back. Only when he was inside, out of Marshall's sight, did he let his shoulders drop. His heartbeat started coming down, too, and he breathed out a small sigh as he came through the kitchen.

"That was painful to watch."

Richard looked up and saw Cruz, Levi King's husband, standing at the window over the sink and eating a sandwich. Levi King owned the Broken Blue ranch and made it a success, but Cruz and Levi were partners in every sense of the word and both of them worked hard to keep it going. "What was?" Richard asked him.

"That little scene out there." Cruz smiled and waved his sandwich at the window. "He was asking you out, wasn't he?"

"No." Richard said. He liked Cruz, considered him a friend, but he didn't want to talk about this right now.

"Then he was about to - don't tell me he wasn't."

Richard just shrugged.

"My question is this - why did you not jump on that?" Cruz shot him a half-cocked grin. He was teasing, but his words were honest, too. "I mean, Marshall is...well, he's something else. He's hot, he's rich, he's smart, he's....I don't know. But it'd be good for you to go out once in a while. What are you averaging now? Fourteen hours or so a day here?"

"Something like that." Richard actually didn't know for sure, but he knew that Cruz would know, because Cruz was doing a lot of the paperwork for the ranch, including personnel stuff like writing the paychecks. "But Sasha needs me, and I don't like leaving her with a sitter."

Cruz clutched his chest with a free hand and rolled his eyes. "You consider Levi and me to just be...." He gasped, "...*sitters?*"

Richard froze for half a second, then grinned and rolled his eyes. "You know what I mean."

"No, Richard. I'm just so wounded right now."

"Shut up." Richard walked around him, got a glass from the cabinet, then bumped his shoulder when he went to the fridge to fill it up with tea.

"Okey-doke. But seriously, Richard, we can watch Sasha anytime you want to go, you know...do whatever. We love having her here."

Richard did know. Levi and Cruz liked watching Sasha even when Richard was right here with her. And they spoiled her relentlessly, no matter how much Richard protested. "Last time, you let her wreck the four-wheeler in the river, Cruz. She was riding alone again."

Cruz frowned. "But she was fine, and she was having so much fun. You should have heard her laughing."

"I heard her scream..."

"Before that. Don't be so truculent. And we made her wear her helmet, like we promised. She didn't even get a scratch."

Richard looked at him. "Truculent?"

"It's my word of the day." Cruz pointed to his calendar. "It means..."

"I know what it means."

"I'm going to tell you anyway, Mr. Truculent." Cruz frowned again. "I might have to shorten that. Mr. Truc...? That doesn't sound right either."

Richard was silent.

Cruz was silent.

"Well?" Richard asked finally.

"Well, what?"

"You were going to tell me what truculent means."

"Oh. It means -."

"Richard! Richard?" Levi came busting through the front door and stopped when he saw them across the large, open-space room.

"Yeah?"

Levi's broad shoulders relaxed when he spotted Richard. "Cal needs your help with Patchy. She's being a pain in the ass again. He says you're the only one who can handle her."

Richard smiled. "Cal's just too impatient. I'm coming." To Cruz, who was glaring at both of them, he said, "I'll be back to hear that in a little while." Then he followed Levi out the door and headed for the corral, where he could hear Cal cussing at one of the ranch's Friesian mares.

When he got closer, he saw that Patchy was bolting every time Cal got too close to her. She wasn't normally like this, not even when she was tired. "Hey, Cal," he yelled. Cal turned, and Richard saw the problem. "Get your ass over here."

Patchy was one of the horses that, until recently, was solely in Richard's care. Each of Levi's hands was assigned three or four, and that hand was responsible for getting them sale-ready. That included daily exercise, getting them used to people and other equipment, training the anxiety out of them and anything else that might turn away a buyer or damage the horse's well-being. But then Levi reassigned Richard to help him with the office work, and Cal inherited Patchy.

Although nobody would know it, since Richard ended up working with her more than Cal did - on top of his regular duties. Richard didn't normally mind, he sort of missed being out with the horses instead of making deals with the likes of Marshall Nivens, but he was also grateful for the raise and the trust Levi put in him.

He climbed over the four-board fence instead of going around to the gate, then hopped down and met Cal halfway across the corral. Cal was tall and a little soft along the shoulders, in spite of the work he did here. He looked like he spent his evenings on the couch, with a hot pizza and a bottle of beer for company.

Reaching down, Richard snagged the halter out of Cal's meaty hand. Cal's jaw dropped. "What'd you do that for?" he asked.

"You're scaring the hell out of her with this thing." Richard snapped. He shook it and let it drop to the ground like a dead snake. "You know she hates it, and you know which one is hers."

"Hers is still wet from being scrubbed this morning," Cal snapped back. "And she needs to get used to wearing different kinds of tack. Her new owners aren't going to have a super-special halter just for her."

They probably would, to be honest. These horses cost more than some houses, and they often got spoiled in their new homes. Sometimes they were treated better than family. "I was in the process of training her when I let you have her," Richard reminded him. "I showed you how to do it."

Cal shrugged. His face was getting red, making the gray bits of his beard stand out. "Well, that's stupid. She can wear this."

"Let's see you walk around in shoes all day that are a half size too small. Would that be good?"

Cal didn't answer, but his lips thinned to a tight line.

"She's a good horse, Cal," Richard said, lowering his tone. "Healthy and strong. She just needs a little special care, that's all. She gets anxious, and then you can't do a thing with her."

"Tell me about it," Cal grumped.

Cal had been around the Broken Blue for as long as Richard, but he gravitated toward the heavy labor - building fence, repairing barns, working with the equipment - more than he enjoyed the finesse it required to handle the big horses. Normally, Levi would have found someone new for this job and left Cal to his strengths, but the ranch was short-handed, as always. "You can't force your will on these animals," Richard said. "You just can't. They're like kids, it'll backfire every time."

"That's when you bust their -."

Richard stepped up then, into Cal's face. He controlled his voice, kept it low, but emphasized every word. "You ever lay a hand on one of these horses and you'll be in jail so fast your socks'll knot. Is that clear?"

Cal opened his mouth to answer, but then he turned and stalked away, across the corral, slamming the gate behind him. Richard watched him go, then picked up the offending halter and dropped it outside the fence, where Patchy wouldn't notice. Then he dug a couple of sugar cubes out of his pocket and went to soothe her and put her away for the night.

Her solid black body was trembling, and her nostrils flared until she heard his voice, cooing to her. Slowly, she walked over and took the sugar he held out to her. Sugar wasn't the best for horses, but he couldn't help it. She loved her *super cubes*, as Sasha called them when she was small.

"Because you're a super girl, aren't you Patch?" he murmured, leading her out of the corral and toward the barns. He loved that his presence made her feel safer, the same way Daddy made Sasha feel safer. He might not have some whirlwind romance, like Levi and Cruz, but he was doing all right, most of the time.

Along the way, he decided he'd made the right decision by choosing to blow off Marshall. His life was all right just the way it was.

He was coming out of the barn, getting ready to head for Sasha and home, when a strange truck pulled into the driveway and stopped in front of the ranch house. It was nearly dark, and headlights flashed off. He saw legs drop down from the driver's seat and then Levi strode out of the house and went to greet the newcomer. Richard hesitated on the way to his own truck, not sure if Levi needed him for anything else, then shrugged and left, waving as he pulled past them. Whatever it was, it could probably wait until tomorrow.

As he drove by, he caught a glimpse of longish blonde hair, faded jeans, wide shoulders and a muscular butt. Something fluttered below his gut, but he ignored it. It was just the effects of Marshall, putting things in his head that didn't belong there.

In other words: Nice, but no thanks. Sometimes Richard got lonely, but he didn't have the time or energy to handle another complication on his life, especially one as unnecessary as a man.

Sasha was waiting for him, and she was the life of his party. Everything else could wait.

Chapter 2

Joey Putnam lit the fuse and stepped back, watching it sizzle above the frosty grass with a grin on his face. Behind him, his foreman Steve let out a whoop and pumped the air with his fist. Steve was drunk, and Joey laughed at his alcohol-induced exuberance. What else was there to do in little bitty Comfort, North Carolina? The only bar was closed down - which was a fact that nearly made his guys revolt before their job ever began. That's why he had to promise them booze and illegal fireworks in some farmer's fallow cornfield just to get them to stay and do the job.

The sizzle thickened and smoke rolled from the short fuse, then the explosive spat itself into the air over their heads. Joey whooped along with the guys this time, laughing as a flock of birds took flight from a nearby tree. The sky flared with red and yellow light. Cardboard casings fluttered to the ground.

"That's it, guys. It's the last one. We need to get back, anyway - it's freezing out here," he said to the five men standing around him. Beyond them, the fields stretched to mountains that rose up in the distance. The landscape was darkening around them, and in another hour he wouldn't be able to see those peaks at all. Man, North Carolina got dark early this time of year.

"We start the job in the morning?" Steve asked. His voice wasn't the strongest.

"No, I still have to find a new man to take Ethan's spot, and tomorrow I'm doing the school thing."

"Good luck finding somebody. Everybody I know thinks our jobs is nuts. Cool, but nuts. They don't want to be wandering around in the woods in the middle of winter." Steve laughed and leaned against the door of his truck, probably to keep from falling.

Joey held out a hand. "Hand 'em over."

"What?"

"You know what. Get in the Expedition, because you aren't driving anywhere tonight."

Steve grunted and dug into his pocket for the keys. It was a pretty standard rule, and they all knew Joey would enforce it. They were a rough bunch, his men, and sometimes their decision-making skills went to hell, but he cared about their safety and made sure they didn't land themselves in too much trouble when they were away from home like this.

He opened up the SUV and tossed Steve's keys into the center console. While the guys climbed in and rearranged themselves to make room, he walked around the area and picked up all their discarded cans and the cardboard bits. When he thought he had everything and his hands were full, he stood up straight and looked towards the sky, shaking his head to get his hair out of his face.

There weren't many stars out so far tonight, and the clouds were low and gray, like they might get some snow later. He hoped so - it would make his job a lot easier if he could track coyotes through snowfall. Of course, this was the south, so he couldn't count on it like he did whenever he worked in the northern states.

He didn't hear any night noises tonight, like the owls or the general rustling of nocturnal critters rummaging through the woods, but that was because the fireworks would have sent them all into hiding.

One of the guys blew the horn, so he turned and headed for the truck.

"Did you meet with the landowner this evening?" John asked him when he was settled into the driver's seat and back on Highway 14.

Joey grinned and glanced in the rearview mirror, catching a glimpse of his own blue eyes before finding John's light brown gaze. He knew what John was really asking - was this job going to be a pain in the ass? Some of the landowners they worked with were downright stupid about inserting themselves into Joey's operation. Usually when that happened, he called the job and left. He didn't need the money so bad, and he wasn't going to put his guys in harm's way because some old farmer wanted to go on the hunt with them. "I did, earlier this evening. He's cool. He knows we're the experts, so he trusts us to handle it. He won't interfere."

"Good."

Joey thought about Levi King and his partner, Cruz. They were the kind of men that Joey respected, because they seemed to be driven by common sense and a general good-natured attitude. Because of that, he felt good about this job, and they didn't even want to bicker about the price, which was a rare and good thing. "Tomorrow I'll do the school presentation, and then in the afternoon I want to take you guys out to scope the place. So sleep it off, all right?"

His men were more like brothers to him than employees. Most of the five had worked with him from the beginning, nearly ten years ago now. They traveled all over the U.S. together, and he knew they had each other's backs whenever something went wrong. Their work wasn't usually dangerous, but under the wrong circumstances it could be, and that was enough to make him wary about taking on anybody he didn't know.

But thanks to Alex's honeymoon, he was going to have to find somebody to pair with Price. He never let his men hunt alone, and this time was no exception. Compared to some of the land they worked, Levi King's property was vast and dangerous, and he would not, under any circumstances, put his guys at risk. So he was going to have to find somebody, but all of his usual stand-ins had other plans.

On a smaller or less important job, he would just shut down operations until Alex got back from Mexico, but this one was crucial to Joey's goals. The King paycheck would put him over the top with his savings, and he'd be free to spend some time back home on the farm he owned with his little brother Mack. He was thinking that taking half a year off sounded good, a break from being on the road all the time. Not that he was going to settle down anytime soon. He was having fun right now, working all over the country, doing a job he loved, growing his business. He knew he was the best in the United States at culling coyote populations, but that didn't mean much until somebody like Levi King said so to his friends and neighbors and his contacts all over the U.S.

In other words, this job would boost Joey's little home-grown company to the next level.

Not that he was struggling now, no way. But he wanted more. He wanted total freedom, and a healthy bank account offered that. He wanted freedom to pick and choose the jobs he took, freedom to take a month or year off if he needed to for some reason. Freedom to blow off work and travel if he felt like it, or go home and spend a month hanging with his brother Mack at the Lucky J down in Alabama.

He suddenly, for just a moment, missed Mack. They hadn't talked for a while, and he needed to call him once he got these guys back to their motel.

The motel they were staying in was the only one in the county, apparently, and it wasn't exactly an amenity-laden wonder. It was more a clean but otherwise nondescript building with two stories of worn but neat rooms, threadbare towels, and one woman who served as the entire housekeeping department, as far as he could tell. She didn't act all that happy about it, either. It did have a neon sign hanging from the office door, which announced that there were vacancies. Joey was pretty sure they never turned that sign off.

But he and his crew wouldn't be here long, and it did what he needed it to do. Also, the price was right, it was less than ten minutes from Levi's ranch, and the guys weren't complaining, so that was a win.

He stopped in to talk to the man who ran the desk after he told his guys good night. Cory Gonzales looked up and gave him a smile when he came in. "Evenin'," Cory said. "Did you meet the semi-famous and rich as God Levi King this evening?"

Joey laughed. He's only been here for a couple of days, but he liked Cory's easy friendliness and happy smile. Joey thought there was a mutual, superficial attraction there, too, but he wasn't sure. It might be nice to have some company while he was here. "Talked to him this evening. He seems like a decent person."

"You met Cruz, too, then. They're nearly always together."

"I did, briefly. Seems like a couple of nice guys."

Cory smiled.

"What?"

"Cruz is an ex-con. Came to work off his parole or something on Levi's ranch, and they fell in love, supposedly."

"Supposedly?" Joey wasn't sure quite what to say. It was just small town drama, and it didn't involve him.

"Well, there are some who say that he tricked Levi, but..." He shrugged. "Who knows?"

"Tricked him?" Levi didn't seem the type to be tricked, from what Joey could tell. They both seemed sharp, and their relationship didn't seem the least bit fake or forced, from what little he'd seen of it.

"Like I said, who knows?" Cory laughed. "If that's so, and Levi ever finds out, then I pity old Cruz."

"Does Levi have a temper?"

"Nah, Levi's the type who doesn't get mad - he gets even."

Joey shrugged off the conversation. It was none of his business, and he didn't much care. "You working all night?" he asked, thinking to get a little quiet time with the engaging and good-looking Cory.

"Yeah, unfortunately. Then I've got to get home and help my dad with some fencing. I tell you what, owning land is a pain in the ass." Cory laughed and tapped the desk with a finger. "I'll never do it."

"Yeah, well..." For some reason, Joey suddenly didn't feel like talking to the desk clerk anymore tonight. He didn't know why, and he didn't care about figuring it out. "I'm going to bed. Catch you later."

He let himself out of the office and started down the walkway to his room, then changed direction and jogged to the end of the lot. Across the street, there was a Rite Aid, and he suddenly wanted a good strong drink. It'd probably put him to sleep, but that was all right. He already had his notes together for the presentation at the elementary school tomorrow, and there would be time for a nap before he and the guys headed out to the Broken Blue.

The drugstore's fluorescents hurt his eyes when he stepped inside, but he blinked it away and headed for the back, where they kept the more common American medicine - alcohol. A shot of Johnny Walker was just what he wanted, now that he'd lost interest in Cory and the possibility of getting laid tonight.

Comfort was just another small town with a bunch of small-town folks, and now he wanted to get the job done, collect his paycheck, and get back to the Lucky J to see the family. He was always welcome there, and he felt like he needed the break. Mack always said he needed to settle down, and maybe once this job was done, he'd think about doing that.

The store was nearly deserted - it was almost closing time - so he paced through and grabbed a pint, a package of small plastic cups, and some chips to munch on before he went to bed. The Kings had offered him a meal when he was there earlier, but he felt guilty about eating roast when his guys were having McDonald's for supper. That meant he was hungry now, though. He checked out, walked back to his room, and locked the door behind him. If any of the guys needed something, they could call. He sat on the bed, put his drink within reach on the nightstand, and flicked on the TV with the remote, leaving the sound off.

His drink smoothed out the evening, relaxing him, so he poured a second just as the phone rang. It was his little brother Mack. "Hey, dude, what's up?" Mack asked when he answered.

"You caught me right before bed," Joey answered, sipping his drink and staring at the silent newscaster on TV. Curiosity nudged his mind – Mack didn't usually call when Joey was out on a job.

"Oh, well, good timing then, right?" Mack paused, and Joey pictured him sitting in the house they grew up in, on the farm they'd inherited from Cusp, the grizzled old farmer who raised them. Mack's curly black hair, so different from Joey's, would be sticking out all over like it always did, and his rounder baby face would be as pale as the moon. Mack didn't tan, no matter how much he worked out in the sun. "Why are you going to bed so early? You never get to sleep before midnight, do you?"

"Sometimes."

Mack smiled - Joey could hear it in his voice. "Maybe Joey the party animal is finally calming down," he teased. "Getting too old."

Joey snorted. "I'm on a job in this little town in North Carolina. I mean, *little* little, man. If not for the Rite-Aid and the Quik Stop, I'd be completely sober right now."

"Oh, man, that's gotta be painful for you. The thought of being sober, I mean."

"Shut up." Joey grinned and swirled the drink in its cup.

"You don't have...uh, company...either, I guess. Otherwise you wouldn't have answered the phone."

Joey heard ice tinkle in a glass on Mack's end of the call and knew he was having a drink, too. "No company tonight. Thought about it, changed my mind."

"You are growing up! I'm so damned proud of you, brother," Mack said. "Screwing your way across the continental U.S. isn't healthy."

Joey rolled his eyes and shook his head at the empty room. Mack was a smart-ass, through and through. "What do you want, ya pest?"

"Just to talk. I hadn't heard from you in a while."

"We've been busy. It's mating season, and you know how that is. Things'll calm down in another month or so, and I'll make a trip down there."

"Good." Mack paused, then said, "There's somebody I want you to meet."

Joey noticed a shift in his tone and sat up, paying attention. "Who?"

"Just somebody."

But there was a lilt to Mack's voice that wasn't there a minute ago. "Do you mean an important somebody? Because it sounds like an important somebody, Mack."

"Yeah, OK. She's pretty important. To me, anyway."

"Is it serious?" Joey asked.

"Um...yeah." Joey listened to Mack's long, long pause. One deep breath. "I got married last week." Mack's voice was steady and quiet.

Joey's mouth fell open. He leaned back against the headboard of the bed. "You...what?"

"Yeah. I mean, we're really happy, but I want you to meet her."

"Whoa, little bro, that's ...wow."

Joey wasn't sure which surprised him more - the news, or the newfound strength in his only brother's voice. Whoever this important person was, she had given him a shot of confidence. He tried to imagine Mack, as shy as a new pup, married, and failed.

"Is she...do you guys live on the Lucky?" he asked.

"Yeah. That's another thing I want to talk to you about."

"What?"

"We want to buy it. Buy out your half, I mean."

Joey closed his eyes and laid back on the bed. That hurt. A lot. "Really? Are you sure?"

"Yes, we're sure."

"Not we, Mack. You. Are you sure this is what you want, and what's going to make you happy?"

"Yep. We've talked about it a lot, and we just want to make it our own, you know? Especially since you're never here."

Another stinger. "All right." Joey sighed, swallowing a lump in his throat. "Let me sleep on it, and we'll talk more in a few days."

He fell asleep an hour later, still wondering what the hell was going on down in Alabama, and wondering if old Cusp would agree to Mack's request if he were still alive. He needed more information before he could make this decision. Mack was too soft-hearted. Joey needed to go down there and make sure somebody wasn't taking advantage of him. It had happened before, and he got the disturbing feeling that it was happening again. Last time, he'd had to go halfway across the country to bail Mack out of jail. This time, it might cost them the family farm.

Chapter 3

Richard picked up Sasha from Pam's house, fed her leftover pizza - her favorite - for supper, and got her bathed and in bed right at nine. It didn't always work out so well, but he was getting better and better at teaching his only little girl new boundaries. The trouble was, her ever-growing mind was always learning new bedtime-avoidance tricks, and he sometimes had a hell of a time keeping up.

She knew it, too. She was a wily little thing. When he tucked her in tonight, she grabbed his hand and asked, "Daddy, do I get to have Blueberry soon?"

Her fingers felt small and soft against his bigger, rougher hands. She was so tiny that he was sometimes afraid to touch her. Not that he was a big man, it was just that she seemed as delicate as the day she was born. "You already have Blueberry, hon." He booped her gently on the nose with a finger. "Levi told you that." He bent down and smoothed the black hair from her cheeks and forehead.

"No, I want her to come here, Daddy. That way I can say goodnight every night."

"Hmm." He bit his lip and looked up, out the window, knowing that he would do anything in his power to make her happy. Maybe someday he would argue with her and try to guide her behavior. Maybe someday he would have to. But for now, he wanted to give her the world, even if he couldn't. And really, there was no reason not to give her this one animal that she loved more than anything else in the world. "All right. I'll see what I can do."

That seemed to appease her well enough, so he started to sing to her, softly, nonsense songs about butterflies and flying ponies. It didn't take him long to realize that not much rhymed with pony and he gave up. After a few moments her eyes fell shut and she snuggled deeper into the covers. He tucked her favorite purple unicorn - incidentally named Blueberry - into her arms and turned out the lights.

It wasn't that he didn't want to give Sasha the horse. They had room, nearly fifty acres of it, and a proper barn. It wouldn't take much to build a decent corral, either. It could be done in a couple of weekends, with some help from the men at the ranch. He knew she'd be responsible for the horse, too. Blueberry was practically her best friend, and she was becoming quite the talented barrel racer at the community rodeos around here. But he wanted to give Levi fair market value for the Appaloosa, and doing that required a little more savings than he felt comfortable giving. He'd planned on buying Blueberry at the beginning of summer, maybe three months from now, anyway, but he couldn't justify cleaning out their savings account for a horse.

Maybe he could work out some kind of deal with Levi.

Her delicate features were becoming more girl and less baby every day. She was a sassy little thing, too, sometimes too sassy for her own good. She often said words that no little girl should know, and he knew it was due to their makeshift family - the men at the Broken Blue, who all spoiled her to death. Sometimes they forgot to censor their language when she was around. She just learned too fast, and he was hard-pressed to keep up with her. It was a proud and heartbreaking thing, watching your kid grow up.

Maybe if her mother was around, it would be different, but somehow Richard didn't actually think so. Unless she had changed a lot, Alicia wouldn't be the best role model, even if she was Sasha's mother. She hadn't wanted kids, and Sasha's birth was a big part of why she'd taken off so angrily and so abruptly, when Sasha was only eighteen months old. Richard hadn't tried to get her back - by then, he knew that she wouldn't come and that even if forced to face the responsibility that Sasha represented, she would resent both Richard and the baby. Things wouldn't have ended as well as they had.

"We get to go to the park tomorrow," Sasha murmured, making him jump. She blinked up at him.

"I thought you were asleep," he said, sitting down on the edge of her bed. He knew they were going to the national forest, because he'd signed off on the permission slip, but he hadn't realized it was tomorrow.

"I'm too excited."

He smiled. "Well, if you don't get sleep, you won't feel well, and then you won't get to go."

That made her wrinkle up her face, even though her head was still heavy on the pillow. "I want to go. Cara is going, and Junie, and Bailey. I need to go too."

He listened to her list off her friends. Some weeks, there were too many little girls in her friends circle to remember them all. He often wondered how teachers kept track. He just hoped they and the chaperones were on high alert tomorrow. A lot could happen in the woods, especially with twenty-four kids to chase around.

"Listen" he said, tapping her forehead gently to make sure she was listening. She giggled. "I need you to be extra careful, tomorrow. Stay within eyesight of an adult the whole time, OK?"

She rolled her eyes. "Daddy..."

"I'm serious, Sasha. You could get hurt. You aren't as grown up as you think you are," he finished, softening the words with a tug at her hair and a smile.

"We'll be careful. We had to sign a promise today."

"Oh, yeah? What kind of promise?"

"That we wouldn't litter. Or go away on our own." She pushed the covers down and ticked off on her fingers. "That we would stay with our buddy all the time. That we wouldn't bring anything that would scare the animals or make them sick. Oh, and that we would listen to the man."

"Those are all good things." He frowned. "What man?"

"The man coming to teach us how to spot an animal in the woods. He's famous."

Richard didn't know they were calling in an expert, otherwise he might have volunteered to chaperone. "Oh, well then...definitely listen to him. It sounds interesting."

"I know. Did you know that we have axe predators?"

He glanced her way. "What?"

"Big animals that could eat us, like lions." Her eyes were huge. Whatever she meant, she was impressed.

He rubbed his eyes and tried to puzzle out what she was saying. Finally he did. "You mean apex."

"Yeah, that."

"Also, we don't have lions here, but there have been possible mountain lion sightings."

"Well, they're lions too. It's right in the name."

He chuckled. "Can't argue with that logic. Just have fun tomorrow and don't get eaten, all right?"

He lowered the lights in Sasha's bedroom and went to get a beer from the fridge, making a mental note to talk to Levi about Blueberry the next morning.

This was the time of evening he dreaded the most. Once Sasha was in bed and not distracting him with her chatter, he felt the weight of the quiet house settle in around him. It would be nice to have somebody to talk to on nights like this, and the thought of Marshall flitted through his mind. He shook it away as fast as it came. Not only did he not want to bring a man in here around Sasha, he didn't want a touch and go fling like the kind Marshall was offering. It would only make things more complicated, and his life was complicated enough. Just thinking about making room for more exhausted him.

Maybe when Sasha grew up and he had the extra time, he'd think about something like that. For now, he was fine.

Bed came early, and he dreamed about things he couldn't remember when he woke up before dawn on Friday. Getting Sasha out the door was like herding a cloud of crickets, the way she was bouncing around, excited to get to school. For once, she was in the truck waiting for him before he finished his first cup of coffee.

He pulled up at the ranch right at six-thirty, looking for any sign of Levi, but didn't see him. Levi liked to ride the fences first thing in the morning, usually starting before sun-up, so he probably wasn't back yet. Sasha snaked her arms into her backpack, kissed him on the cheek, and hopped down out of the truck. He watched her run for the house, where Pam would be waiting with eggs or pancakes, and he sent up a small prayer that she would have a safe day. He didn't know if he could survive the heartbreak if something happened to her.

Pam technically worked for Levi, coming in every morning to straighten the house and cook for the guys in the bunkhouse, but when she had offered to put Sasha on the school bus, too, it had been like a gift for Richard, taking just a small amount of responsibility off his back. Now that he had Sasha he understood the reasoning behind big families all living together and sharing the work.

He was saddling one of the horses, getting ready to hunt down Levi, when the diesel from the night before rumbled down the driveway and parked in front of the ranch house. Two men got out and looked around. Another truck pulled in behind it, and three men climbed out. They couldn't see him in the shadow of the open barn doors.

Richard stopped what he was doing for a moment and studied them. They were average looking guys, and they all looked confident in a way that he used to feel but seldom did these days. They were dressed in jeans and flannel shirts, and even in the snappy cold of the morning, only one of them was wearing a jacket. A couple of them carried sidearms. They gathered around the man who was here the night before, listening to him. Whoever they were, he was obviously their ringleader. He was explaining something, apparently, and they looked when he pointed toward the river behind the house. Then he pointed toward the barns.

He was strikingly good-looking, enough that Richard spent a few appreciative minutes letting his eyes wander. The shoulder length dirty blond hair, his tanned skin, and high cheekbones that framed his full lips and dark eyes, all made him interesting. The hair and tan said surfer, the jeans, boots and holster at his belt said security. The high forehead and cheekbones made Richard think Native American, and his slim but muscular build spoke of an athletic life. The other men looked like they were in good shape, too, but for some reason, maybe just his bearing, he stood out among them.

Richard waited a few beats to see if Levi was going to come back and speak to them, but when he didn't, Richard thought he'd better. Leaving Corona saddled, he led her to the water trough and then went out to see what they wanted.

"Can I help you?" he asked when he got close enough to hear.

All five men turned to look at him, and the leader smiled a little. The smile reached his blue eyes. "Maybe. Have you seen Mr. King this morning?"

Richard shook his head and shifted his feet. The man's gaze was direct and powerful, and Richard's heartbeat jumped a notch, although he couldn't have explained why. "He normally goes riding this early, but he should be back before long. What do you need?"

The man left his friends and came over to Richard. He stuck out a wide, dark hand. "I'm Joey Putnam," he said. "I'm the man who's working with Levi to cull the coyote population here."

Joey moved smoothly, and turned his body in a way that included his men as well as Richard in the conversation, even gesturing toward them. "This is my crew."

Richard liked that - Joey clearly respected his men and considered them part of the situation, instead of just random employees who happened to be standing there.

Richard smiled and shook his hand, but he was trying to remember if Levi had said anything about this. He had, but only in passing, when one of their mares turned up injured a few weeks ago. All signs pointed to a coyote attack, and later they'd found a dead coyote in one of the ravines across the river, its head looking a lot like it had made contact with a sharp hoof before it died. Richard was glad that Levi was working on this.

"Good," he said. "We need it, before things get out of hand around here."

It took a few seconds for him to realize that Joey Putnam was still holding his hand, and that his hand was large and warm. And that contact sent unmistakable heat up Richard's arm and across his shoulders. His eyes met Joey's blue ones and he felt a weight settle between them, some pull that drew him toward the new man. Joey felt it too. His eyes widened a fraction and his smile grew into a lop-sided, sassy grin.

The temperature was near forty and the sun hadn't even begun to kiss the sky overhead yet, but Richard suddenly felt hot. He nodded and pulled his hand away, even though he had to force himself to do it.

He turned away from Joey and the men, who were watching this exchange with casual curiosity, and pretended to scan the area for any sign of Levi. Inside, he was mentally shaking his head and trying to get his heartbeat under control. What was wrong with him? He didn't react to anyone like this, much less a perfect stranger. Maybe it was the unexpected nature of meeting him in the swirl of morning mist. Maybe Marshall's advances were still planted in the back of his mind, because this was definitely a visceral sort of attraction - not one he planned on pursuing, of course, but he couldn't deny it was there.

He heard a thin grumble of noise in the distance and relief washed over him. Levi. He took a steadying breath and turned back to Joey Putnam, who was looking at him intently. "Here he comes," Richard said, offering a smile. "Riding the fences is part of his regular morning routine."

That last was unnecessary, but he needed to speak, to put some damper on whatever just happened between them. "Are you men hunting today? I'll need to move the horses."

Joey shook his head and shoved his hands into his pockets. "Nope, I just came out to show these guys the general area. You know, let them look around, and introduce them to Levi. Later I've got a date with a bunch of second graders."

Oh. Richard nodded slowly, putting two and two together. "I believe one of those second graders is mine. She mentioned having an expert come to teach them about axe predators."

Joey's forehead wrinkled. "Say that again?"

Richard laughed, his tension easing away. Just talking about Sasha made everything a bit better. "It's a long, silly story. Just know that she and her friends are very excited to meet you."

Joey still looked uncertain, but he said, "Good to know, I guess."

"You must like kids, to offer to do something like this."

Joey shrugged. "I do, I guess. I don't have any of my own, but when they're around they seem to like me. Mostly I want to teach them to respect the outdoors and stay safe whenever they find themselves around a wild animal."

Thankfully, Levi came around the barn. His ATV engine drowned out any need for further conversation, and all six men turned to watch him pull up and park.

"Mornin'," he said, climbing off the machine. "Good to see you here so early, but I thought you wouldn't start until tomorrow."

Joey explained what he was doing, speaking easily to Levi. The other men listened in and Joey introduced them.

Richard turned to go inside. "Good to meet you guys," he said, "But I've got to get to work."

Levi raised a hand and gave him a wave, but Joey spoke up. "Hold on a minute. We might need your help, if you're open to it."

Richard had no idea why they might need his help, and he did have things to do, but mostly he just wanted to get away from his uncomfortable curiosity about Joey. He forced a smile and said, "Sure."

Levi cocked his head toward Joey. "Let's get inside, out of this cold. My face is starting to hurt."

Chapter 4

J oey didn't miss his own reaction to the man named Richard, but he didn't welcome it, either. He was here to do a job and then get out, not find a surprise attraction to some random employee at the King ranch. Sometimes that was fun, a little distraction during an ongoing job. Sometimes it was just what Joey needed to take the edge off his tension and finish up whatever job he was working. But Richard was a complete stranger to him, and Joey got the distinct feeling that he wasn't a casual hook-up kind of guy. Talking about his kid sealed it. Richard was off-limits. Joey didn't need complications, and serious relationships caused complications.

Those thoughts were all true, but that didn't stop his gaze from wandering back toward Richard whenever Levi was talking to him. The man was well-built, solid, with a steady gaze and a bit of a swagger in his step. His smile, when it appeared, was a little self-deprecating, which made his dark good looks even sexier. And he had more of a twang to his voice than Levi, which Joey definitely liked.

In another time and place, Joey would absolutely be interested.

Price was walking closest to Joey as they followed Levi into the house. He kept shooting Joey a snotty grin that Joey knew all too well. Was his immediate interest in Richard that obvious? He hoped not. He was here to do a job, an expensive one, and he didn't want Levi King to think he was getting sidetracked by a sweet piece of ass, especially by one of Levi's own employees.

He still let his eyes slide lower when he followed Richard up the porch steps and into the house. Once inside, Richard said something to Levi that Joey didn't hear, and that made him look up.

"Well, come on back when you're done. I want your input on this," Levi said to him, at the same time he was ushering the men through the room to a long oak table.

The house was warm and softly lit. Joey liked that - he hated harsh lights or too much noise first thing in the morning, preferring to ease into the day. The room was huge and open all the way across the front half of the house, and encompassed the living area, with lots of leather furniture. There was an abundance of white-painted wood, and a fireplace made of what looked like locally sourced stone. Mack would fall in love at first sight with the dining room area and the bright kitchen. There was a lot of leather in here, and the house was decorated in mostly neutrals - gray and cream, stark against the mahogany colored leather and stone. It created a stable, soothing atmosphere, a lot like the vibe he got from Levi himself. He and his guys settled in around the table while Levi went to get coffee.

"This is a nice place you got," Price said as Levi set a steaming mug of coffee down on the table in front of him.

"Thanks. My sister hired somebody and they did it together." Levi smiled and took a seat across from Joey.

Joey liked that - not many men understood the importance of face to face interaction, but Levi did. Joey did too - he preferred to look a man in the eye, and it was hard to do that sometimes. He never trusted a guy who was always looking away, looking at his phone, or doing something when Joey was trying to talk to him, especially when he was trying to talk about large amounts of money. His services didn't come cheap. Everyone seemed to be so preoccupied all the time that trying to get anything done was often irritating at the very least.

That was one of the reasons he loved his job – he could party with the best of them, and did, but he also liked the solitude of walking a trail or settling in against a big tree in the quiet of the morning.

Once Levi was settled, Joey introduced each of his men. He could hear Richard in the other room talking to someone, maybe on the phone, and he was annoyed with himself. He wasn't here because of Richard. He was here to get a job done for Levi, and so far it sounded like it was going to be a pretty big job. Maybe as many as twenty coyotes in this local pack, which was rare but not unheard of in Joey's experience.

"We've been hearing the coyotes a lot lately - almost every night. When they get going," Levi said, "It sounds like this place is surrounded."

"Has anyone been feeding them?" Joey asked. "Some people do, either thinking they're dogs, or maybe just because they feel sorry for them. It's winter, and some people have a soft spot for these animals."

Levi shook his head. "I know none of us are, but maybe someone on one of the neighboring farms? What do they eat, anyway?"

Joey shrugged. He was in his element now, talking about the one creature that he understood better than any other - even humans. "They'll eat anything - mostly rodents like mice and rabbits, but they've been known to eat garbage or fruit. Of course, deer is always on the menu, but it would have to be a fairly large pack to take down a deer. That sounds like what you've got, if they are brave enough to try to take down a horse."

Levi nodded, listening intently.

"Have you noticed any disturbance in your grain supply here? They'd have to be pretty hungry to eat it, but I've seen it happen before."

Levi shook his head. "We keep the grain sealed in drums. Otherwise, we'd lose a lot to mice. I can show you if you want to look around."

Joey shook his head. "Nah, you'd definitely notice if they were getting into it - they're messy animals. Like I said, they usually go after mice, so they're actually helpful in some ways. A big pack like yours will help with the deer population, too."

He looked at Levi and waited. It didn't happen often, but sometimes a farmer actually called off the hunt at this point, usually because they grew crops instead of horses. In that case, the songdogs could actually be helpful, if deer tended to eat into their yields. But he didn't think Levi would do that, because for him, his men, and his livestock, the coyote were a danger. Joey had done the research on Levi - his horses were worth plenty. Levi wouldn't risk them.

Richard came in through a doorway near the kitchen and grabbed a cup of coffee. His eyes found Joey's first, although his expression was unreadable. Joey thought he looked...not apprehensive, but maybe somewhat guarded. His smile was a little tight, too. Joey smiled back. For some reason he wanted to put Richard at ease, maybe see a real smile light up the man's face. Richard looked like the kind of man who wore his emotions freely.

Joey found himself wanting to see if that was true.

But that wasn't why he was here, and that sly grin from Price told him that he wasn't hiding his emotions right now, either. He shook off his interest in Richard and nailed his attention on Levi.

"I have a bit of a dilemma," he said. "It's nothing I can't fix, but I'd like your input."

Levi nodded for him to continue and listened, sipping his coffee.

"Is this the part that involves me?" Richard asked.

"Maybe." Joey glanced at him, then looked at Levi again. He hoped he wasn't making a mistake. Now that he knew Richard had a kid, he wasn't sure this was the best idea. It was too late now, though. "Right now we're a man short, and I don't like sending my men out alone to hunt. Instead of three teams, we're at two and a half, and I need another half. Can you recommend somebody local? Somebody you know who can handle firearms and not be an idiot in the woods?" He turned to Richard. "I didn't know if you'd be interested."

"Maybe..." Levi said slowly, thinking. He was looking at Richard, though.

Richard turned to him. "I'll do it," he said.

Levi frowned.

Joey frowned. That was fast.

Price's grin widened.

"I mean, if you don't mind," Richard said, looking at Levi. He came over and took the last empty seat at the table. "Everything is caught up, and I think it sounds interesting."

Joey had kind of hoped Richard would turn down the job. Coyote hunting could be dangerous. At the same time, he felt stupid for worrying about it - Richard was a grown man, so he would know if going on a hunt like this was a good idea. It wasn't Joey's place to judge a man's intentions, much less his abilities. And it would solve the problem.

Levi didn't look any happier about it than Joey felt. "Why? I mean, I'm sure we can find another man, so you don't have to do this, Richard."

"I know you can, and honestly I wouldn't, but as it turns out I've been given marching orders from the young one."

Levi grinned at that. Joey found himself smiling, too, even though he wasn't sure what they were talking about. He assumed the young one was the child Richard spoke of earlier, but what did that have to do with this?

"What orders?" Levi asked.

Richard ran his hands through his hair and sighed lightly. "She's so stubborn."

"That's what makes her cute," Levi said with a laugh.

Richard shot him an exasperated look. "Well, she's gotten it into her head that you're going to sell Blueberry, and she wants me to buy him - *right now, Daddy. Pretty, pretty, please please please.* So I'm going to need the extra money."

Levi's booming laughter filled the room, loud enough that Joey had to grin, too. Even Richard smiled.

The sound brought Levi's partner Cruz in from the hall. His lighter looks complemented Levi's well. They made a good couple. He looked like he hadn't been awake long. "Oh, good morning, guys. I didn't know you were here," he said, walking behind Joey to get a cup of coffee from the pot.

Levi made quick introductions, and Joey was impressed that he remembered the names of all five of his men without any prompting. Every time he interacted with Levi, he was more and more impressed with the man and his operation here. His curiosity was growing where Richard was concerned, too, even though there was no reason for it and at this point he was actively trying to fight it. The last thing he needed was to get involved with a family man.

"You know, I'm sure, that things can get dangerous on a hunt like this," he said, looking across at Richard, who met his gaze openly. There was that weight again, that thickness in the air, drawing Joey toward Richard's presence. He cleared his throat. "Not that I'm judging you, but you said you had a kid, so you might want to think about that."

He was very aware of his men keeping their eyes on him. They didn't like the locals working with them on a job, and normally Joey agreed with them, but it was better than waiting two weeks for Alex to get back to work, especially now that Joey had to get home to see what was happening with Mack.

Richard nodded his acknowledgement, then turned to Levi. "In lieu of payment, I'd appreciate it if you could consider this a down payment on the horse. I'll pay off the rest next week."

Levi frowned. "You don't have to get all formal about it, Richard. Of course, we can work out whatever terms you want. Hell, you can take Blueberry on home and pay me later if you want."

Richard was already shaking his head. "No can do, boss. You know that. I'd rather buy him outright than take on debt."

"You planned to do that anyway," Levi said. Then he grinned and said, "The only reason I haven't insisted you take him on home is because we like having Sasha here on a regular basis."

Richard grinned, too. "You think I don't know that? Y'all spoil her rotten."

Joey watched them talking, noting the warmth between the two men, and appreciated it. Some places he worked, you could feel tension or outright ugliness between a landowner and his employees. It made everything about the job less pleasant, and it also told Joey exactly how he and his men would be treated if something happened during the work. He didn't like working for surly men, and he was almost in a position to turn down that kind of job when he encountered it. He was looking forward to the freedom.

"You're welcome to join us," he said, "If you're sure. Like I said, we do our best to keep things safe, but these are the woods - you never know what could happen."

Price spoke up. "We lost one guy when he broke an ankle jumping across a creek. He messed himself up pretty bad and never did come back to work. We lost another to snakebite." He shook his head. "You just never know."

Richard met Price's gaze full-on. "The same thing could happen to me here, doing my regular work. I've been thrown off horses so many times I've lost count, and there's always some job that could go bad if a man's not paying attention. I guess it's part of the job, whatever job you do."

Price nodded. "Right, right. Just so you know."

Levi got up to get more coffee. As he walked past the large, gleaming oak kitchen island, he reached out and gave Cruz's arm a squeeze.

Joey had almost forgotten Cruz was still standing there, he was so wrapped up in the enigma that was Richard. That told him he needed to get this - whatever this was - out of his system. Later, he'd find Cory and take him up on his offer of some casual nighttime distraction. That would hopefully do it. For now, though, he needed to concentrate. He watched Levi come and sit back down, then he looked at Richard again. "If you want, you can come along with us today," he offered.

Levi said, "I thought you weren't hunting today?"

"We aren't, but like I said, I want to show my guys the lay of the land here. We do it everywhere, just in case there's trouble and they need to get out of the woods in a hurry. Of course," he nodded toward Richard, "You know this place pretty well, so you don't need to do that, but maybe you can help us out."

"Sure, sure." Richard nodded. To Levi he said, "I've got to schedule payment to Marshall this morning and then put a hold on the new beams for the river, like you wanted. Anything else before I head out with these men?"

Levi shook his head, but then he shot Richard a grin. "You sure you don't want to hold off on that payment?" he asked, his tone teasing. "Marshall might come back looking for it."

Richard groaned. "Stop it. That man is going to drive me to my grave if he doesn't find a regular boyfriend soon."

Levi looked at Joey and explained, the smile still on his face. "One of our suppliers has the hots for Richard here, and he doesn't want to take no for an answer. Myself, I think they'd be cute together."

"Marshall isn't cute. He's a nuisance," Richard griped. "I've told the man no a thousand times."

In spite of himself, Joey's interest piqued. So Richard was definitely open to a male-male relationship, just not with this Marshall dude.

Interesting. That is, if he was interested himself. Which he wasn't. At all. Richard was in it to buy a horse for his kid. Joey was in it to get the job done safely and efficiently. That was all.

So why was he both excited and apprehensive about Richard accompanying him into the woods?

Chapter 5

Richard watched the men file out the door, talking quietly. Now that the introductions were over and everybody was on the same page, they seemed more relaxed.

Except for the man named Joey, for some reason. If anything, his face held more tension than before, and Richard had to wonder if it was because he was coming along on the hunt. Joey appeared to take his men's safety very seriously, and Richard was a wild card with a gun, as far as he was concerned. Richard could see that being cause for some trepidation.

He didn't like that he was getting distracted by Joey, though. If he was being honest with himself, that moment between him and Joey was interesting, and Richard had to admit that he was curious about the man. He shoved his hands into his jeans pockets and went back to his office to take care of business, knowing that Joey was waiting for him outside.

Hopefully, going on a hunting trip would get all the extra testosterone out of his system and he could go back to being a boring old family guy.

It didn't take long, a call to the bank to release payment to Marshall, and then a call to the lumber company to hold the beams that were scheduled to be delivered the next day - the crew leveling the riverbank wasn't ready for them yet. It was all day-to-day business as usual, but for some reason that Richard didn't want to think much about, he felt lighter and more optimistic than he had in a long time. He refused to believe Joey had anything to do with that, but he was having trouble coming up with any other explanation, so he shoved the whole subject out of his mind.

Maybe it was just the idea of a change in his duties. Every man needed a little something out of the ordinary once in a while, right?

Joey Putnam is definitely out of the ordinary, isn't he?

Richard shook the thought out of his head. Enough of that. His hands were full with Sasha, and he didn't know anything at all about Joey. The whole exchange might have been all in Richard's imagination. And even if he was gay, he was a single guy who traveled the country for work, and it didn't take a genius to understand that his lifestyle was probably a lot different than Richard's. It had to be, otherwise Joey would most likely have settled down somewhere by now.

He told himself all this as he handled his work, grabbed a coat, and started toward the front of the house.

Cruz was in the kitchen, wearing a red and white checked apron that covered his clothes and doing something to a hunk of bread dough. It smelled amazing - yeasty and warm - and Richard's stomach growled. He ignored it. Cruz looked up when Richard came through and smiled.

"Going out to play with the boys?" he asked, laughter lacing his voice.

Richard shook his head and rolled his eyes. He was used to both Levi and Cruz teasing him about his dates, or lack of them. "Just paying for Sasha's very expensive taste," he said.

"Wait. Richard," Cruz held out one floury hand and Richard stopped. "You know it'd be good for you to get out a little, if you're as interested in that Joey guy as I think you are."

"I'm not." Richard started to walk away, but Cruz's snort stopped him. "Yes you are," said Cruz. "It was all over your face. It's good, I'm glad." His smile softened. "Levi and I worry about you sometimes. You need grown-up friends, too."

"Nah, I'm good." Richard shifted from one foot to the other and glanced toward the door. "Sasha and I do all right. And we've got you guys."

"I know, believe me. You're the best dad, and I know how much she loves you." Cruz looked toward the door, and then met Richard's eyes again. "But maybe you should think about blowing off a little steam for yourself once in a while. You know?"

Richard didn't know what to say to that, so he just nodded.

Cruz studied his face for a moment, then widened his grin. "Bring Sasha by for supper tonight." He nodded toward the ball of dough. "I'll make her some cinnamon rolls."

All right, I will. Y'all spoil that girl," Richard said for the third or fourth time this morning.

Cruz laughed out loud. "We know. No need to thank us for it."

"Later," Richard said and escaped out the back door before Cruz could say anything else about his love life. Cruz was still laughing when the door closed between them.

Joey and Levi and the others were standing near the rear bumper of Joey's truck, chatting, when Richard got to them. He met Joey's eyes briefly, then looked away, toward the mountains. "Ready when you are," he said.

"Are you not taking ATVs?" Levi asked, a hint of surprised curiosity in his voice.

"No. If it was snowing heavily we would," Joey explained, "But mostly I like to keep it on foot. ATVs tend to scare away the animals we're hunting."

He spoke to Levi, but his eyes remained on Richard. "By the way," he said, "Did you get those maps I need?"

"Oh, sure. Hold on." Levi turned and jogged back into the house. Richard was able, finally, to break eye contact with Joey to watch him go. He emerged a few moments later with folded sheets of paper. "These should be a lot more detailed than the ones I sent you before," he explained, handing them over to Joey. "Although Richard here knows this land like he knows his own face, so if you have any questions, I'm sure he can help."

"I'm sure he can," Joey said, his voice low.

Richard looked at him. Joey was still looking at Richard, something unreadable in his eyes. Richard didn't take the time to try to figure it out. He was suddenly too hot under his coat, even in the cold morning air, and he wanted to get moving before his own thoughts got out of hand.

Price, standing nearby, made a noise that sounded a lot like laughter and turned away. Joey shot him a look, but didn't say anything.

"We'll cover this end of the valley, then work our way down and across the river in general," he told Levi. "If Richard will give us an idea of where you're hearing the most activity, that'd be perfect."

"That all right with you, Richard?" Levi asked. "I've got to get busy."

Richard nodded. "Could you have a couple of the hands check the fence in the northern pastures?" he asked. "I'd like to move the horses down there if we'll be hunting that end, just to be on the safe side."

"Yep. Good idea. I'll get Cal to do it, since he can't handle Patchy," Levi said with a laugh.

Richard grinned and watched Levi climb on his four-wheeler and take off toward the hay barns. Then he spun in a slow circle, looking up toward the surrounding mountain tops. "If I remember correctly," he said, pointing upward. "We heard them just a couple of days ago, near the orchards."

Joey nodded. "Good start. Was it early morning, or -?"

"No," Richard interrupted. "It was just after nightfall. We were here late, having supper with Levi and Cruz. It fascinated Sasha, and she didn't stop talking about it for the rest of the night."

"All right. Any other time?"

"One of the hands, Cal, reported them several times on Friday night. Oh, and Sonny found tracks on the riverbank near the house he shares with our foreman," Richard said, trying to remember.

"When was that?" Joey asked. He unzipped his jacket and pulled a pen from an inner pocket, then scribbled something onto the maps Levi had just handed him.

"Not sure, but I think it was pretty late. We were teasing Cal about needing a curfew because he looked rough, but he blamed it on the coyotes keeping him awake."

Joey looked up, eyebrows raised. "They came in close enough to wake up your men?" he asked. "That's pretty rare."

Richard shrugged. "Maybe they were hungry. We've been keeping the horses closed up at night since our mare got injured."

"Did he say if they were out in the open? Or in the woods?"

"I don't think he did. Want me to ask him?" Richard asked, shuffling his feet in the frosty, glittering grass. It looked sharp, glistening in the first rays of sunshine peeking over the mountaintops. It was going to be a beautiful day, once the sun came up.

"Nah, we'll figure it out." To his men he said, "We're going to spread out a little. Keep an eye out for tracks and scat, but don't get too far from each other until you feel like you know your way out again. I've got..." he checked his watch, "About three hours until I have to head for the park for the kids, so split up, figure out your game plan, and let me in on it before I go. All right?"

Richard liked his tone of voice, liked the way he gave his men instruction but didn't harp on about it. He trusted these guys, Richard could tell. It was like he knew they could do the job, and he was turning them loose and letting them do it. Some men - usually insecure men who didn't know or trust their own authority - couldn't do that. They had to micromanage and intrude into every decision, no matter how small. They had to insert themselves into every possible conversation, too. Richard was happy to see that Joey wasn't like that.

"When we get back into town this afternoon, remind me to make copies of this for each of you," Joey said, waving the maps.

"You need copies?" Richard asked, glad to contribute something. "I can do that."

He held out his hand and Joey gave them over.

"Be back in a minute," Richard said and turned to go inside. He was glad to take the moment alone, truth be told, although he could feel Joey's eyes on him all the way to the house. Waiting for the copier, he pulled out his desk drawer and took his holster and .357 Magnum from its space there. Strapping it through his belt felt oddly out of place, and he realized that it had been a long time since he went out to shoot targets. He vowed to do that more often, just to keep in practice.

He blew out his breath and decided to get control of himself - he hadn't even known how tense he was just now until he got away from Joey. That kind of tension caused mistakes, and he really didn't want any mistakes during this thing. He wanted to help Levi, do the job he promised Joey he would do, and get Blueberry home to Sasha. Everyone would be happy, and he could relax and put these new, disturbing thoughts out of his head. He didn't want a relationship, he didn't need one, and he didn't have time to even entertain the thought. Sasha took all of his time and energy, and he liked it that way.

Forget that Joey's eyes on him felt warm and curious. Forget that he was excited about this hunt. Forget how long it had been since he'd felt this kind of interest in a man. None of it mattered. none of it was life changing. All of it was a distraction, compared to what really mattered. His daughter, his simple country home, and his work here at the Broken Blue. Those nights when he felt that twinge of lonely, quiet solitude were just tossed pebbles in the river flow of his life.

Sasha was the rapids. She was the screaming laughter, the rush of love and joy, and the clear path ahead when everything else was steep sides and rocky shores. He had no business thinking about something that would disrupt her life, so he decided, on the spot, that he wouldn't. Joey was just another ranch hand - temporary, skilled, and here to do a job. He would be gone in a couple of weeks, if not days, and Richard could go back to thinking about what was important.

For a brief moment, anger stirred in his throat, making it raw, but he didn't know why and he didn't have time to care. The copier beeped that its job was done, so he grabbed the paperwork and headed back outside, where Joey and his men were waiting and talking casually.

"You ready?" Joey asked, taking the papers and giving Richard another of those unsettling once-overs. He raised an eyebrow when he spotted Richard's side arm, but didn't say anything.

"Yep. Let's get this thing done," Richard replied, keeping his voice clipped and his eyes averted. He fished a pair of gloves from one of his coat pockets and shoved his hands into them.

Chapter 6

The woods were probably Richard's favorite place to be. Probably because some of his best childhood memories stemmed from the forest, hunting with his own father and, later, hanging out with his friends, going camping and hiking on the many beautiful days of his teen years. These days, he didn't get out here as much as he liked, and hunting had almost become a thing of the past for him. There was simply no time, and it wasn't a necessity, so he had let the hobby fall by the wayside, and the trade-off - time with Sasha - was fine with him.

He was surprised that Joey and his men didn't come fully armed. The weight of his own gun made him notice, and a couple of the other men were carrying, too, but Joey wasn't, and no one seemed too worried about going into the woods unarmed. He mentioned it to Joey as they made their way up the farm road toward the head of the valley. Now that he'd made his decision about not getting involved with Joey, conversation came more easily to him and the tension between them had burned off with the early morning mist.

"These guys consider carrying weapons their job," Joey explained. "They don't carry unless they feel the need, the same way you don't carry a halter and lead rope unless you know you'll be working with horses. Some people are uncomfortable in the woods, but we spend so much time out here that we're used to it, I guess."

"Is there a huge demand for this?" Richard asked, genuinely curious. Until Joey walked onto the scene this morning, he didn't even know there were companies that did this work, and he said so.

"Enough to keep us busy." Joey went to the soft edge of the graveled road and scanned the sandy, leafy litter. Richard wondered what he saw. A man trained to track animals judged everything differently than someone like him, who only went out into the woods and made his own marks instead of reading what had been there before. His grandfather had been such a man, but Richard had never picked up the skill for some reason.

The other men had gone on ahead, talking about the terrain and pointing here and there. Now Joey came back to walk along beside Richard. "See that ravine?" he asked, pointing toward a skinny wash that meandered upward toward a jagged crevice in the massive capstone of the mountain. A small trickle of water ran down toward the river below. "Coyotes love spending their nights in there, waiting for prey to come in for a drink. They'll often den right in that area, too. It's near the water and, like I said, plenty of food. It's protected too, and not much could sneak up on them in there."

Richard nodded. It made perfect sense. "Then why do they ever come out?" he asked. "Why not just stay put and let dinner come to them?"

Joey nodded, as if he knew Richard would ask that question. "A smaller pack of three or four might do just that. Lone coyotes do it that way, too, especially if they're in another pack's territory. But big packs, like the one I suspect you have, are another story. They can't survive on a few mice and squirrels. They need to come out and hunt larger prey, or they start to starve."

"Like deer," Richard said, understanding. "Or horses."

"Exactly," Joey said, pointing at him. "I'm honestly surprised you haven't come across more deer carcasses lately."

"We might, if it were summer. We tend to keep the live-stock - and the men - in closer to the main ranch during the winter. This river can get too dangerous sometimes, and we can't risk losing either human or equine lives."

"Makes sense, and it's probably why you haven't lost any animals. How long have you been hearing the songdogs?"

Richard smiled at that. "I like that you call them songdogs," he said. "It makes them sound like they're special animals."

Joey cocked his head. "They are special animals. Wily and quick. They're incredibly smart, too."

There was real admiration in his voice. He glanced up and smiled at Richard. "So now you're wondering how I can like them and still kill them, I guess."

Richard shook his head. "No - I understand."

"The population becomes unhealthy if it gets out of hand. I don't like to see them starve. I don't like them on the highway, getting hit by cars, either. Too many people and coyotes get hurt that way."

"So you do what you can," Richard said, earning a soft smile from Joey.

"I do what I can," Joey agreed. "It just happens to be lucra-tive."

"That's good."

"I suppose." Joey pointed. "See that?"

Richard looked, but there was nothing there. Just trees, some of them evergreens, and farther on, the river. A few rocks. "What?"

Joey put a hand on his shoulder and steered him toward the side of the road. Pointing to one of the long-needled firs, he said, "That. Coyote fur."

Richard saw it now. A reddish gray wad of soft, silver-flecked hairs, caught underneath one of the low branches, around knee level. "A young one?" he asked.

"Maybe." Joey didn't touch the fur. "It could have been an adult taking shelter under here, too." He got down on his hands and knees and disappeared under the lowest limbs. "Aha," he said after a few minutes, backing out. He held up what was left of a small mouse, as best Richard could tell.

"Not much of a meal, was it?" Richard asked.

"Barely a snack, I bet." Joey chuckled and tossed the small body back where he found it, then got up and brushed off his knees. "That was the only one there, too. We'll have more luck farther into the woods, I think. Away from the barns and maybe closer to the orchards."

Richard nodded. He realized that the other men had moved farther ahead, and now they were disappearing into the woods along the fence line, although they remained together in twos. Joey didn't say anything, but he seemed to be keeping a casual eye on them, maybe making a mental note of where they went into the trees.

"You worry about them?" Richard asked, nodding ahead.

Joey shrugged. "I shouldn't. They all know what they're doing, and I'd trust any one of them with my life - and have, for that matter. But I still worry. Too many things are unpredictable, you know?"

"Oh, hell, do I know."

Joey looked at him for a moment, then grinned and nodded. "Because you have a kid," he said.

"Right. Every time she steps out the front door, half my brain is on full alert, even though - like you said - so much is completely unpredictable. Do you have kids?"

"Nope, but I get it." Joey nodded, his gaze brightening. "Although I'll never admit to these guys that I worry about them. I'll never hear the end of it."

Richard didn't know if all fathers felt that way, but he was surprised that Joey understood the feeling so well, since he wasn't a father at all. "Whenever I tell Sasha to be careful, especially in front of her friends, she rolls her eyes at me and shakes her head. She has no idea."

It felt odd, talking to this guy, who was basically a stranger, about Sasha. He didn't tend to share too much where she was concerned - you never knew who might be listening. Call it paranoid, but he didn't take chances with her. But Joey didn't feel like a risk. Actually, Richard hadn't even thought before sharing with Joey about his little girl. Weird.

They walked quietly for a while, with Joey pointing out more tufts of fur that Richard would never have seen on his own, and once he even pulled Richard over to outline tracks in some mud near a spring. He touched Richard casually, like a buddy, and Richard's response every time was to just about burst into flames. He tried to be casual about it, tried to make himself relax. It had been too long, he decided, that was all. He didn't like that he felt so suddenly starved for companionship, but he wasn't about to do something about it right now. Besides, what could he do? Kiss Joey, out of the blue, here in the cold woods?

Very dramatic, but completely out of the question.

"You all right?" Joey asked, making Richard look up sharply.

"Yeah, I'm fine. Just thinking." He wasn't going to explain what he was thinking about.

"If you don't want to do this, I understand," Joey said. "Some people just don't like to hunt. I get it."

Richard blinked. "No, it's not that..."

"And those early mornings are going to be pretty tough, I guess, since you've got a kid."

"I..." Richard stopped. "Early mornings?"

"We head into the woods at three in the morning. We need to get settled before the coyotes start coming into their den."

"Oh. I didn't know that."

"Is it a problem?" Joey seemed to be trying to talk Richard out of it.

Richard would have let him, if not for the promise of Blueberry and the look on Sasha's face when he brought the horse home to her. "No, it's fine."

He would have to get Pam's help to get Sasha off to school, and Sasha wouldn't be happy about it, but he didn't really have a choice. "It's fine," he said again. "I can make arrangements. When do we start?"

"First thing in the morning. I've got business at home to handle, so I need to finish this job up quicker than I'd like."

There was something tight in Joey's voice when he made the comment about home. Richard wondered if there was a story there, then decided it was none of his business. He shook his head and led the way toward the orchards, noting that none of the other guys were anywhere in sight now. The chill in the air was icy on his exposed skin, and the sun was coming up soft and bright, making it a beautiful morning.

When they reached the orchards on top of the mountain, that effect was amplified, giving the day a golden glow that bathed the rows of apple trees in warmth. It felt good on Richard's skin, and Joey's too, considering the way he stopped and stretched tall. His lean body was graceful and dark against the winter sky. Richard looked away.

Joey looked around for a few minutes, then said, "I bet they love it up here - plenty of open space, lots of critters coming for the fruit - or what's left of it."

"We've heard them howling and yipping from this direction before," Richard answered, "So you're right about that. I thought they stayed down in the hollows, though, so it didn't occur to me that they might be up here."

Joey nodded. "They do stay in the hollows when they rest, but this is prime hunting ground - like I said, lots of little critters up here for them to feast on at night." He turned and walked closer to Richard. "You say you haven't seen them close to the house?"

Richard shook his head. "No. Sasha - that's my little girl - plays there. If we'd spotted them near the house, I would have started shooting them myself."

Joey's eyebrows came up. "You hunt?" he asked.

Richard shook his head. "Used to, but I haven't gone hunting in a while. Not since Sasha was born, at least."

Joey nodded, as if this confirmed some guess he had already made. "You're comfortable doing it now?" he asked.

"Sure. I just don't know a lot about the habits of coyotes. You know? I can tell you how a deer will act, or a turkey. I know where they'll turn up, I know where to aim for a clean shot."

Joey let out his breath.

"What?" Richard asked.

Joey squeezed his shoulder, but there was a hint of fire in his blue eyes. "I'm glad to hear you say that, about making a clean shot. It makes me angry when someone only wounds an animal, leaving it to suffer."

Richard frowned. "I bet...who does that?"

"Oh, you know. Good ole boys who are in it for the fun." He shrugged. "Drunks. You run into all kinds in the woods, you know?"

Richard shook his head. "I guess I don't. I've always hunted on private land, and usually alone."

"Count yourself lucky. I've met my fair share of dangerous individuals." He paused. "The state of Maine hired us one year, and I swear we met the craziest people up there. One of my guys nearly got shot because his cap was the wrong color orange."

"Uh...but it was orange?" Richard wasn't following.

"Yep. Just a slightly darker shade. Apparently that means it's fair game for gunplay. In Maine, anyway." Joey chuckled.

"Wow."

"Another guy, who had been too close to a bottle for most of the day, from the looks of him, wanted to buy my truck, pay me cash right there in the woods and let me and my men walk out. He'd killed a deer and didn't have a way to get it home. This was in Ohio, I think."

"Why wouldn't you bring your truck if you were going to kill a deer?" They'd been walking slowly between the rows of trees, and Joey scanned the ground as he walked. Now he stopped and looked up at Richard.

"He wasn't - that was the funniest part. He'd gotten drunk at some local bar, then gotten lost when he was walking home and ended up in the woods. Since he had his .44 strapped to his hip, he decided he might as well kill something."

"Jesus," Richard said softly. He crossed his arms over his chest and leaned against a tree, noticing how easy it was to be comfortable in Joey's presence, now that they were getting to know one another. He reminded Richard of Levi in that way - you knew he'd come down hard if necessary, but otherwise he was as easy-going as they came. Richard liked that a lot. He also liked hearing Joey talk about his work – his voice came easy and there was a hint of pride when he talked.

"Yep. So I don't have a lot of patience for dangerous or cruel individuals." He looked out toward the sky and the valley that dropped away below, then shrugged. "You don't seem to be either of those things, so I think we're good."

Richard realized he was staring at Joey, the way his jaw set against the white and blue sky, the way his body moved as he looked around and took stock of the area. He was a sensual man, Richard could tell, a man who experienced the texture of the world in a way that most men didn't. He seemed to revel in the soft breeze, the bright sky, the crunch of the grass under their feet. He reached out to touch the bark of the young apple trees as they passed or feel a dry leaf between his fingers. It was fascinating to watch and Richard found himself wanting to feel those things too, wanting to reach out and touch.

Except that what he wanted to touch was Joey. The dark skin of his jaw. The way his longish blond hair would run through Richard's fingers. The hardness of his chest and the way his thighs might flex under fine tawny hair.

Richard fell on his face, barely catching himself with one hand. Pain shot through his wrist and he yelped and grabbed it as he scrambled back to his feet.

Joey was reaching out to help him. "Are you all right?"

Richard pulled away, leaning against a tree trunk to help his balance. His face was hot, more from embarrassment than anything. "Must have been a root or something," he muttered, keeping his eyes away from Joey and rubbing his forearm, which throbbed a little from the impact.

"Did you hurt yourself?" Joey asked, stepping close enough that his coat brushed Richard's. "Let me see."

Richard thought to turn away, but he wasn't fast enough. Joey had his arm and was pushing up the coat sleeve. His warm breath touched Richard's cheek, and Richard's entire body flamed as hot as his face.

"I don't think it's sprained or anything. You might have a bruise." Joey's fingers pressed lightly at the tender inner hollow of Richard's wrist and Richard trembled. He still wanted to pull away, but his body wanted him to lean in, to feel the length of Joey's body against his own.

He swallowed hard. "No, I think it'll be fine," he said, his voice too deep. He cleared his throat. "Just clumsy."

Joey finally stepped back to a respectable distance, and Richard felt cold. "Got to pay attention in the woods," he quipped with a lop-sided smile.

"Yeah. For sure." Richard looked around, trying to think of something, anything, to change the subject and get Joey's attention off him. "So we come up here in the morning?" he asked. "For the coyotes?"

"No." Joey shook his head. "They'll be headed down the mountain when we get here, going to their den for some day-time sleep."

"Then where do we wait?"

Joey walked to the edge of the orchard, and Richard followed along behind until they stood at a fairly steep drop-off. Below, between the top of the mountain and the houses and barns in the valley, stood a thick stand of trees and the river. Richard could hear it flowing from here.

"Probably there," Joey said, pointing to a ravine that cut away to their right. Richard could barely see it through the shelter of trees. "It's deep enough for them to den safely, and far enough from the farm road that equipment won't bother them. That's my guess, anyway. I could be wrong."

"If you are?"

"Then either the other teams will find them, or we'll come back the next day. We can't take more than three a day anyway."

Richard frowned, still looking at the ravine because he was afraid to look at Joey again. This time he might fall off a cliff and kill himself. "Why three?"

"Because when we start shooting, they'll scatter. When we stop shooting, we want them to come back. Too many dead coyotes and they'll leave for safer territory. Who knows where they'd end up, and that would just be pushing the problem onto somebody else's land."

"Oh, OK. Got it." Richard paused. "I hope I'm not asking too many stupid questions," he said after a moment.

"Nope. I'm glad you're asking. A lot of men wouldn't." There was warmth in his voice. He reached out and squeezed Richard's shoulder again. Richard put his hands in his pockets to keep from reaching up to touch him.

It made him angry - at himself. What was wrong with him? He wasn't that starved for affection, was he? He had gone for a long time without adult attention, so why were his hormones going crazy today, of all days? It was stupid, and he gave himself a mental shake, trying to snap out of it. Joey was here to do a job, not date Richard, just as Richard was here to earn Sasha's horse, not get laid. This was business.

The thought of Sasha was like a bucket of cold water, clearing Richard's mind. "Well, I guess we start in the morning, then."

"Yep. If you're sure," Joey said, giving him an odd look.

"I'm sure. Let's go."

Chapter 7

Joey texted his men that he was leaving, got into his truck and left the Broken Blue. They'd be busy walking the land for most of the afternoon, probably, scouting for the best vantage point. It was like a contest for them, to see who could bring home the best kill for each job. They were respectful enough, and the contest kept them enthusiastic about working, so Joey didn't mind. He even offered a cash payment sometimes, just to keep the competition alive.

Meanwhile, he had a date with a bunch of elementary kids, but what he really wanted to do was examine his reaction to Richard. Something had happened back there, he just couldn't yet say what it was. It was attraction, sure, but not the usual passing appreciation that marked most of his encounters. This was something more subtle, but at the same time more powerful than he'd ever felt.

Every time Richard's gaze found his, or when he looked up and caught the color rising in the man's cheeks, he wanted to reach out and make contact with him. It was almost as if his hands had ideas of their own, and Joey had to fight hard to keep himself in check. Otherwise he would have pushed Richard up against one of those trees and smothered him with kisses, because those full, dark lips were just begging to be tasted.

A couple of times there, Joey had to reach out and touch something - anything, a tree, a leaf - just to keep himself grounded in the real world and keep his mind from spinning away into fantasies about what he and Richard could do together. He'd been fighting it all morning, and now he was drained, but he still had to get to the park and hang out with the kids for a while. Hopefully, they'd be energetic and curious enough to keep his mind off...whatever.

The park entrance was rustic and hard to miss. It was also hard to miss the line of bouncing kids headed to the visitor's lodge at the far end of the parking lot, where he was supposed to meet them. The sunshine was bright, even if the air was cold, and they were all bundled up in colorful coats and toboggans with puffballs on top of them. He parked, got out of the truck, and grabbed a canvas bag from behind the seat. Then he waved to the teacher that looked up when he slammed and locked the door.

She met him halfway across the gravel lot and offered a pale hand for him to shake. "Glad you could make it," she said, smiling brightly. "The kids are excited to meet you."

"Great. Can't wait to get started," he said, holding her elbow and steering her toward the lodge doors.

The kids were inside now. She looked at him like she wasn't sure if he was being rude, and he couldn't explain that he wasn't, not without sounding like a crazy person. He was just nervous. Not because of the kids, but because of her. He'd never been good at one on one communication with women - teachers, neighbors, any of them. His brother Mack said it was because he had no experience - their parents took off so early that he could barely remember them being there at all. Joey thought that Mack might be right about that, because no matter how hard he worked at it, women still terrified him, especially if he had to spend any time with them alone.

It occurred to him now that, instead of running from Richard, he should have invited him along. Richard probably knew these people well and he would have acted as a buffer of sorts. It was too late now.

"Is something wrong?" the teacher asked. What was her name? He'd seen it in the emails, but he hadn't paid attention.

"No, ma'am, I'm fine. Just...going over what I want to tell the kids."

She laughed lightly as he pulled open the glass door for her. "You don't have to call me ma'am. I'm Carolyn."

"Carolyn." He smiled. The ma'am trick hadn't let him down yet - it worked every time.

It was slightly warmer inside the lodge, at least, and out of the wind. The sun shone on the gleaming wood and tile, but didn't make the large room feel any more homey than the average office space. Several benches made of live-edge logs filled the room, and a pull cord hung from the top of one wall for a projector screen. The information desk in one corner held stacks of brochures for possibly every tourist trap in the state of North Carolina. The kids were gathered mostly in a different corner looking at a large stuffed, realistic-looking bear. They oohed and aahed over it, and one little boy with a shock of black hair reached out gingerly to touch a paw that was as big as his head.

"Alex!" Carolyn called in a sharp voice, making Joey jump. "No touching!"

Alex jerked his hand away and a couple of the other kids laughed. He stomped over and sat down on one of the log benches.

"Guys, come over here, please, and say hello to our guest," Carolyn called, waving the rest of the kids toward the logs.

They came, reluctantly, wanting to stay and look at the bear some more. Joey didn't blame them - the animal was beautiful, and he didn't want to imagine meeting one like it in the woods.

Carolyn stepped between Joey and the kids, near the front of the logs. "OK." She clapped her hands. It echoed a little. "Does anyone remember this man's name?" she asked.

Silence descended on the room as everyone looked at Joey. Some of them shook their heads.

"This is Mr. Putnam. Can anyone tell me what he does?"

Several hands shot up. One of them belonged to a wiry little dark-haired pixie that had to be Richard's daughter. No question about it. Her features, her skin tone, and her dark, dark eyes were all his. When she turned her gaze his way, he couldn't help but smile.

He pointed at her, interrupting Carolyn the teacher. "You," he said. "What's your name?"

"Sasha," she said. Her voice was firm, not the least bit timid.

"And you know what I do for a living?"

"Yes." She squirmed in her seat, as if she suddenly realized that she was in the spotlight. That didn't stop her, though. "You're going to work at the Broken Blue where my dad works, hunting for the coyotes."

He nodded. "Yep, you got it." He reached into the canvas bag and pulled out his secret weapon - a Hershey's Kiss. He tossed it to her and she caught it with a grin.

Carolyn, standing off to one side of him, frowned.

He didn't care - kids loved candy, and the promise of it always made these talks a success. He wasn't going to quit because one lady was uptight.

"All right," he said. "Who knows the most interesting fact about coyotes?"

Not as many hands shot up this time, but it didn't matter. The boy named Alex shouted, "They turn into werewolves during the full moon!"

That made Joey laugh, but it didn't earn Alex any candy. "I wish - they'd be more fun that way. OK, who can tell me a real fact?"

Another hand shot up, this time a little blonde girl in a hair bow and a frilly dress that was destined to be in tatters by the end of a day in the woods. "OK, you." He pointed at her.

She put her hand back in her lap. "They can run really fast. My dad said fifty miles an hour."

He smiled and gently lobbed candy in her direction. "Almost. Your dad is mostly right. If they're chasing their food they can go forty-five, but only for a couple of minutes. Then they get too tired. Does anyone know what else can go forty-five miles an hour?"

Several of the boys shouted at once, "A car!" A motorcycle!" "Superman!"

Joey snorted and grinned at Carolyn, who smiled back but still didn't look happy about the candy thing. What was her problem, anyway?

"OK, whoever said car is pretty good - a car can go a little bit faster than that, but you're close. For the record, I have no idea how fast Superman can fly. Maybe it's forty-five, too."

He tossed a Kiss to the boy who answered car, and a small noise from the teacher made him look at her again. She said, "Hold on, kids, while I talk to Mr. Putnam for a moment." Then she motioned him over.

Suddenly he was nervous again, but he came over and bent down so that she could speak quietly into his ear. "Jared is the boy in the red striped shirt," she said.

"Okaaay..." Was this some kind of weird code?

"He's allergic to peanuts. You can't give him any candy."

Oh. Joey frowned. Crap. That's what she'd been so upset about. "Shoot. I'm sorry." Now poor Jared would feel left out, even if he answered a question right. "What do I do?"

She blinked and didn't answer. Obviously, it was his problem to figure out. Maybe Jared wouldn't know any of the answers. Maybe. But that was wishful thinking and not a solution to the problem.

He thought for a moment, then said to the kids, "I'll be right back." Then he jogged out to the truck and opened the glove box, praying he was right about it's contents.

He was, and relief washed over him.

Five years ago, he'd decided to quit smoking. The only way he'd been able to pull it off was to suck on one of the old-timey Dum-Dum suckers. All day, every day, for months on end, he had one of those things sticking out of his mouth. After a few weeks, a couple of the other guys decided to quit, too, and for a while he was buying the dang things in bulk.

As it turned out, that was around the same time his business started to really take off, and a small superstitious part of him made the connection. Since then, he put a new bag of the suckers into his glove box before every job, partly for good luck and partly in case he was dealing with somebody who made him want a cigarette. It didn't happen often, but here and there he got the urge, so he was always ready with a sucker handy.

Hopefully, this was good enough. He checked that the bag had that little peanut disclaimer on it - it did - and shoved some into his pocket. Then he jogged back inside, giving Carolyn a wink as he took his place in front of the group. She didn't relax any.

"All right," he said. "Back to it. Who can tell me what coyotes eat?"

While he was talking, he pulled a folded poster from his canvas bag and opened it up. Then he fished around for some tape and hung it on the wall behind him. The kids' attention instantly went to it, and he saw a few eyes go wide.

The poster was one of his favorites, portraying a coyote at the pinnacle of a snow-covered mountain top, holding a rabbit in its mouth. At the coyote's feet were two small pups, looking up at her expectantly.

He turned back to the kids. Three of them had their hands up, but as they studied the poster, more hands raised. He pointed to Richard's daughter. "Do you know?"

"Horses," she said, her voice firm. "One of ours got bitten."

He smiled. "Well, they'll try to eat a horse if they're in a big pack, or if they're really, really hungry, but usually they stick with smaller meals."

Her face screwed into a frown as she thought about this. He pointed to Jared, the boy in the striped shirt.

"Mice," he said. "And maybe birds?"

Joey smiled at him. "Good. Definitely mice, and maybe birds, but those are pretty hard to catch."

"Maybe if one was hurt," Jared suggested. "You know, laying on the ground, like if it fell out of its nest."

"Yep. They would probably eat that poor bird."

Carolyn was wringing her hands in front of her and staring hard at Joey. He gave her a wink, then pulled a sucker from his pocket and held it up.

Her face cleared and she gave him a little nod. He tossed it to Jared, who missed, smacked it, and yelped when it went sailing toward the back of the room. Then he ran for it. Joey waited until he was back in his seat to get on with it.

"Do coyotes eat squirrels, too?" A little boy asked. He was one of the smallest kids in the class, with freckles and clear blue eyes behind his glasses.

"They do, if they can catch them." He looked at the boy, and then the others. "Why do you think a coyote might not be able to catch a squirrel? Does anybody know?"

"Because they can climb trees, silly!" Richard's daughter said. Then she paused. "I mean, the squirrels can climb trees, not the coyotes."

The whole class laughed at that, and Joey was relieved to see that she laughed, too.

"OK, now, does anybody know where coyotes live?"

This time he got a chorus of answers.

"The woods!"

"The park near the river!"

"Behind the mall! I saw them!"

Joey chuckled. He was having fun, mainly because Carolyn seemed content to stay out of the way and let him do his thing. He hated it when teachers tried to run his talks. He spent the next few minutes telling the kids more about the animals he respected so much, until he saw that they were getting tired of sitting there.

"All right," he said, laying Kisses and suckers out on the table in a row as he talked. "One more question. What is the most important thing to remember about coyotes?"

"They'll eat your cat!" one child called out.

"They're fast!"

"They have sharp teeth!"

"All right, all right. First of all, they won't eat your cat, or even get close to your house, unless they are really, really hungry. Did you know that a bunch of scientists checked scat for nearly a thousand coyotes and only found one ca-."

Alex piped up, "What is scat?"

The rest of the kids looked at him expectantly. He glanced at Carolyn, who shrugged. She looked amused, like she was enjoying his discomfort now that he wasn't about to accidentally kill one of her students.

"It's..." He tried hard to think of a better word, but nothing came to him. "It's actually poop."

The whole class burst into *"Eew!"* mixed with laughter. He grinned.

"Wait a minute!" Richard's daughter said loudly, enough to get everyone's attention. She glared at him, suspicious. "You mean it's somebody's job to look at poop?"

He nodded. "Yep. It sounds gross, but a lot of times that's the best way to find out about a wild animal, since they're so good at hiding." Then he grinned, "All right, who wants to be a poop detective when they grow up?"

That brought more wrinkled noses and laughter and teasing from the kids. "Everybody come on up, get some candy, and check out the cool stuff I brought to show you. You did good."

He emptied the rest of his bag, laying out casts of coyote footprints, a small pelt so they could feel its fur, and a few teeth in a jar. The teeth were always a crowd favorite.

That was one of the reasons he liked to talk with younger kids - they still got excited about the same things that excited him. High school kids were too cool to show enthusiasm, and they tried to act like everything was just a big stupid joke.

He watched as Jared stood at the table, sucking on a sucker, but looking sadly at the silver Kisses scattered there. After a moment, Richard's daughter came up to the table. She reached for one of the Kisses, then paused and glanced at Jared with an unreadable expression on her face. Then she grabbed a sucker, too, and stood beside him while she ate it.

Joey smiled at her, but she didn't see it, so he gave them time to look at all the goodies and then took them outside, into the trees, where they spent a while looking for coyote tracks and guessing at good places a coyote might make its den. The kids had lots of great questions, and some great jokes, too. He was happy and exhausted when he was back in the truck and headed for the motel.

He was halfway there when Richard crossed his mind again. He had managed to avoid thinking about him for the last few hours, but now his curiosity was back in full force. He clicked on the radio and tried to ignore it, but it didn't fully work.

There was just something about the man...Joey didn't know what it was, but he wanted to know more, especially now that he'd met Sasha. She seemed to be a great kid and a genuinely nice person, like her dad.

Why had he acted so skittish when Joey was just checking his wrist for injuries earlier? Richard was an outdoorsman, definitely - he moved through the woods and along the trails with confidence and knowledge. So why did he get all nervous when they were standing in the orchard? Why wouldn't he look at Joey when they were talking? Joey had seen the apprehension on the man's face, but where did it come from?

He didn't know, and he wasn't likely to find out, so he tried hard to just forget about it. That meant stopping by the drugstore on his way to the motel and buying something stronger than the juice box Carolyn had offered him.

He took it home, checked in with the guys to get their game plan for the next morning, and then considered stopping by the office to see Cory. But halfway there, he realized that he just wasn't interested, so he left it alone and went on to his room to mindlessly surf the crappy TV.

Chapter 8

At three the next morning, he and his men were standing in front of the Broken Blue's main ranch house. He watched Richard's truck pull in and park. He climbed out, grabbed a Thermos, slung his rifle over his shoulder, and walked through a few swirling snowflakes to get to them. His footsteps were loud in the early morning quiet.

"Mornin," Joey said, his voice coming out too loud in the still air.

Richard looked at him and rubbed his hands together. "It's a cold one," he said. "You know it's winter when the mud gets crunchy." Then he held up the Thermos. "I brought coffee, but I forgot cups. There's some in the bunkhouse, though."

The men declined. A few of them had brought their own supply. "We ready?" Joey asked, his breath riding the air. "Sign off on the map."

He pointed to a map on the hood of Steve's truck, held down by a pair of gloves and a screwdriver. It was segmented into sections of land and Richard watched each man write his name into a wedge - the one they would be working. "It's a just-in-case sort of thing," Joey explained as he bent to write his name. "You're with me, if that's all right."

Richard nodded and signed in, then stood back and caught the two-way radio Joey threw at him. "Everybody ready?" he asked.

Richard nodded along with the others.

Joey had half expected Richard to not even show up. It was a cold, slightly snowy morning, too early for most. Even the stars stayed hidden behind a thick blanket of fat clouds this morning, and Joey bet there'd be some significant snowfall by the time they rolled in later this morning.

He and Richard took the same road they'd taken the day before to get to the orchards. "I met your daughter yesterday," Joey said. "She's a cute kid."

Richard chuckled. "She couldn't stop talking about the field trip yesterday. You did a good job with those kids. I haven't seen her this excited about school since the beginning of the year." He paused. "I do have one question, though."

"What's that?" Joey knew they were going to have to quiet down in a minute, but he was glad to hear that that kids liked him.

"What on earth is a poop scientist?"

If he hadn't been very aware of how much noise they were making, Joey would have laughed out loud. "I'll explain later," he said. "It definitely made an impression on the kids, though."

"You got that right. She wouldn't stop talking about it."

Richard stopped talking after that, and they made their way up the mountain in near silence.

Joey loved mornings like this, and he was happy that he could walk along beside Richard and feel comfortable in the silence. Some men couldn't do that. Some men - people in general, really - had to always be talking or making noise. He wondered how those people ever had time to think. He was pretty sure he'd go crazy trying to come up with something to say all the time.

They were about halfway to the orchard when Joey stopped, tapped Richard's shoulder, and pointed off into the woods, toward the skinny trail he'd spotted the day before.

Leaning in close, he whispered. "I think that if they're in our section, they'll den in the ravine we saw. Let's get over there and get settled."

Richard nodded and turned in that direction. For a while, they picked their way through denser underbrush and ducked tree limbs, until Joey saw a hollow that would work. It was a small rock outcropping set into the trees a little. Beyond it, the trees thinned and the area opened up for about fifty yards, leaving the perfect clearing. If coyote had a den in the ravine, they were going to come this way, so they almost had to cross through this clearing.

He pulled a small flashlight from his coat pocket and flicked it on to be sure. "Here," he said, pointing, then pulling Richard's sleeve until the man followed him that direction.

Kneeling down, Joey duck-walked back into the hollow, until his back touched the rocks. After he was settled and had the light pointed toward the ground to minimize it, he motioned to Richard, who did the same thing. The light allowed them some small measure of sight in the inky darkness, but it was enough.

Once they were as settled as they were going to get, Joey wondered if he might have made a mistake. Richard was very close, nearly pressed against his side, and he found it to be a bit...distracting. This wasn't like him - he was here to do a job, not play footsies with the local talent.

Normally he was able to separate those two things pretty easily, but not this morning. Instead of listening to the woods, he was listening to Richard's breathing. Instead of honing in on any movement in their surroundings, he was thinking about the heat Richard's body was giving off. Every inch of him tingled, and he felt his jeans tighten.

Damn it. Concentrate, you asshole.

"What?" Richard whispered.

Joey winced. Had he spoken out loud? "Nothing, sorry."

He was about to shift his weight a little, minimize the contact, when he heard the unmistakable sound of a snuffling coyote, not too far away. He nudged Richard, put a finger to his lips, and cupped his ear with his free hand. Richard turned his head and listened, dropping his jaw the way the way Joey had seen some of the old-timers do when they wanted to hear better. Then he glanced at Joey and nodded, a soft smile on his lips.

Joey stared at that smile for a beat too long, but then he heard the crackling of small paws in dead leaf litter. He picked up his rifle as carefully and quietly as he could.

Richard shifted a little to give him room, then prepared his own rifle for a shot. Joey liked his confidence with the weapon, and liked the respect and care Richard used when he handled it. Richard was just sighting down the barrel when Joey caught movement from the corner of his eye, off to his left.

He didn't know it, but he must have made a small sound, because Richard froze.

The songdog that stepped out from the brush, about a quarter of the way around the clearing and so far oblivious to them, was a young female. Her eyes flashed briefly as she turned her gaze their way, but she didn't bolt. Not yet. Coyotes were skittish, sometimes more easily startled than deer, and anything could send them running. That was part of why Joey enjoyed the job - every scenario was a different challenge.

Slowly, as carefully as he could, he reached into his pocket and pressed a button on the small box there. The resulting squeak, to his relief, brought the coyote a step closer. Her ears were alert, curious about the noise.

Unfortunately, at the same time, Richard jumped and let out a little gasp.

The coyote was gone in an instant, fading quickly into the brush and away. He heard her running through the leaves and grunted.

"Oh, hell. I'm sorry," Richard was whispering. "I didn't know you were going to use a call."

The look of devastation on his face made Joey feel guilty. He answered without bothering to whisper, because their girl was long gone and she probably wouldn't be back anytime soon. "No, you're right. I should have warned you. I just didn't think about it. We always use calls of some sort, and I assumed you knew, when you didn't."

Richard was still frowning, and Joey suddenly wanted to get that expression off his face. The thought irritated him - why should he be so worried about the momentary discomfort of a near-stranger? He was here to do a job, and he needed to do it. Hell, Richard wasn't even complaining, he was taking the blame.

Joey forced himself to relax and resettle himself in the hollow. Richard was a grown man, and he would be fine. "We'll have to move in a few minutes. They might not come back this way today," he explained.

Richard started to apologize again, but Joey held up a hand. "Stop. Like I said, my fault. Just know in the future that I will be using calls, and that coyotes will disappear faster than you can blink at the slightest sound or smell. They're smart critters, and they've lived in the woods a lot longer than us." He smiled, and finally Richard smiled back and turned to fully face him.

"I guess I'm so used to working with my crew that I didn't take your experience level into account," Joey continued.

"Yeah, well, I don't have any experience with coyotes, and it's been a long time since my deer hunting days," Richard said.

"I get that." Joey was just glad that Richard didn't seem to be feeling bad anymore. "Besides, we got really lucky. A lot of the time, I can sit still for an hour or more and never see a coyote."

"Even when you're using the calls?"

"Sometimes especially then. Like I said, coyotes are smart, and they've been hunted so much in some areas that they have no problem telling the false calls from the real thing. Calling coyotes is kind of an art, even with the best equipment." Joey turned the light to illuminate more, then pulled the call box from his pocket and showed it to him.

"What kind of call was that, anyway?" Richard asked, leaning in to look at it.

Joey felt the heat of Richard's arm against his, and they were close enough that he could feel Richard's breath on his cheek. It shook him, that closeness, and his heart did a strange little lurch, like it had been waiting for exactly this moment.

He took a deep breath and answered the question. "This one is a coyote pup in distress," he said, pressing the button again so that it repeated the squawking yip. "I've also used injured rabbits, other coyotes, interrogation howls, invitation howls...the list is pretty big."

"What's an invitation howl?" Richard asked.

"A female in heat."

"Aah. I can see how that would work..." Richard looked down at the gray and red plastic box. "It looks sort of like an old walkie-talkie."

"It does but it's invaluable in this line of work. All of my men carry one, and I could almost say it was the cause of our success."

They were quiet for a moment and then Joey continued.

"Fawn calls work, too," Joey said. "A lot of people see it as cheating to use these little machines, but those people usually go home without a kill."

Richard laughed, and Joey suddenly didn't want to hunt anymore this morning. He wanted to go back to the house and talk to Richard over a hot cup of coffee. He wanted to hear Richard's opinions about...well, everything. Looking at Richard as he inspected the callbox, he wanted, very badly and very suddenly, to kiss him.

He stood up fast, almost knocking the box out of his own hand. "Come on. They won't be back here, so we need to find another hiding spot."

Chapter 9

Richard couldn't believe he did something so stupid, and it reinforced and brought to the surface an idea he'd been ignoring for a long time - he was soft.

It was a hard thing to swallow, and it left a bad taste in his mouth. He had grown complacent and soft, there was no way around it. He loved his life and he loved Sasha, and he wouldn't change any of that for the world on a platter, but at the same time, he'd lost so much in exchange. He used to be a good hunter. He used to be decisive and quick. Before he married - against his own better judgment - and had a family, he was stronger, faster, and more daring than a lot of men. He worked hard, he played hard, and he remembered all of it.

Now, here was a guy that lived all the things Richard used to be. Joey reminded him of his wilder, tougher days, and in a lot of ways Richard missed that. He missed taking off on a four-day hunting trip, only coming out of the woods on day five because he had to get back to breaking horses. He missed the thrill of sighting in on an animal and making the kill, bringing it home to feed one of the local families. And he missed the adrenaline rush of all the close calls he'd lived during his active life.

Now he had Sasha, and he didn't take chances. The stakes were too high. What would happen to her if he got injured, or worse, died? Would they hunt down her mother, who saw Sasha as nothing more than an inconvenience and was perfectly happy to leave her behind? He shuddered at the thought as he followed Joey through the woods. Would Cruz and Levi take her, since they were her godfathers? They probably would, but it was irresponsible to do that to them when they were still finding their own life together.

Besides, he couldn't imagine a greater pain that losing his little girl, under any circumstances. Even death.

So he couldn't regain his wilder days, but he knew, after meeting Joey, that he had to find a way to get back to that fearless part of himself and live his life. Because the truth was, he'd been hiding behind Sasha. He'd been using her as an excuse, in a way, to settle into a safe and boring routine. That wasn't who he was, and it wasn't who he'd envisioned when he was young and thought about getting older. Not that his thirties were old, but he was sure acting like they were.

He grimaced at his own thoughts and shook his head. Such a deep existential crises, all because he jumped at an unexpected sound.

"What?" Joey had turned to glance at him.

"Nothing, just thinking about something. No big deal." Joey turned and kept walking. It was a big deal, though, Richard thought, maybe because he'd ignored the signs for so long, thinking that he would fade gracefully into middle age and be just fine.

He could do that, but now that he'd met Joey he simply didn't want to. Compared to Joey, Richard hadn't been living - he'd been existing. And now he wanted to live again. It was an ache in his belly, one that he'd been ignoring for a long, long time.

Joey stopped walking and looked around, and Richard wondered what he was thinking. He'd always heard that coyotes were notoriously difficult to hunt, but Joey didn't appear to be worried about it. In fact, here in the early morning frosty forest, he seemed to be in his element. Maybe it was something in his voice, or maybe just his presence, but the excitement was there, and it was almost palpable.

It was clear that Joey loved his work. As a plus, he apparently respected the land and the wildlife, too. Richard found that admirable.

Sexy, too.

He shook that thought away.

"Are you all right?" Joey asked.

"Yeah, I'm fine." Richard hoped Joey would stop asking, because he wasn't about to try to explain his thoughts. They barely made sense, even to him, so how could he make a guy like Joey understand? He knew one thing - he had a lot of thinking to do, and he was going to need time and guts to do it.

Not now, though. Right now, he'd promised to do a job, and he was determined to do it and do it right. Luckily, Joey was a natural teacher.

They walked downhill at an angle, moving through thick trees with low-hanging branches and coming slowly closer to the ravine. A couple of times Richard heard a lonely howl on the other side of the mountain, and a few yips here and there in answer. It was a haunting sound, one he wouldn't want to encounter out here alone and unarmed.

Joey stopped and waved him forward. Richard walked to his side and looked at where he was pointing. "Scat," Joey said.

"Yep." Richard glanced at it, then looked away. But hadn't he just been thinking about toughening up? If the sight of poop made him queasy, he might as well hang up any hopes of being an outdoorsman again. So he looked, and took note of how it looked, in case he ran across it again.

"Why did I think it would just look like dog poop?" he asked.

Joey shook his head. "Dogs eat what we give them, so theirs is soft. If you were to look, you'd find plenty of bones and hair in this."

"No, thanks," Richard said. It was good information to know, but he didn't want to get up close and personal with it.

Joey chuckled and looked around a little more, shining his light farther along the ghost of a path they followed. "Check this out," he said. This time he knelt to brush away some leaves.

Richard knelt beside him. "Tracks," he said.

"Yep. See how they go in a straight line? Dogs would wander around sniffing at stuff. Coyotes do all their exploring far, far from the den, so when they get close they're ready to head home. So..." his gloved finger followed what he was seeing. "Straight line."

After he pointed it out, Richard could see it too, but mostly he was struck by the excitement and barely contained pride in Joey's whole demeanor. The man's hand hovered close to the ground, and there was a smile in his voice. If nothing else, Joey was a good teacher because he was definitely passionate about the subject. No wonder Sasha had been so excited when she got home yesterday.

Richard didn't know much about Joey or his background, but he knew one thing - when Joey was in his element like this, he was attractive as hell. "How would a man get into this line of work?" he asked. "It's fascinating."

Joey chuckled. "Well, you could come to work for an outfit that's already established, like mine. I guess you could do what I did and find an old-timer who was willing to teach you all the ins and outs, too, although those guys are getting harder and harder to find these days."

Richard grinned. "You'll be one of those guys someday," he said.

Joey made a face. "Good point. Hopefully it'll be a while before I hang up my hat completely."

Richard nodded. "And then what will you do?" he asked.

Joey shrugged. "Well, my brother Mack and I inherited some land in Alabama," he said. "A good bit of it, too. I always thought I'd go back there when I got tired of the hunt, but now I'm not sure."

"Why not?" Richard was genuinely curious. He wanted to know more about Joey and what made him tick.

Joey stood up. "My brother just got married. He wants to buy me out."

Something in his tone made Richard think he wasn't happy about it. "You don't like that idea?"

"It's not that. He called me out of the blue and..." He paused and looked away. Shuffled his feet a little in the leaves. "It was a surprise, that's all."

Richard was surprised to see Joey looking uncertain. "I get it. You suddenly have to decide what your own plans are worth."

"Exactly." Joey smiled. "Not so easy to do."

"I know. Levi offered to sell me part of the Broken Blue once. Not a lot, but enough that I was invested."

"You turned him down?"

"Yep. I wanted to build my own thing, you know?" Richard put his hands in his pockets and shot Joey a rueful grin. "Some days I wonder if I made the right decision."

"You happy?"

Richard ignored the thoughts that had been gnawing at him for the last hour. "I am, for the most part."

"Then you probably made the right decision." Joey dropped a hand on Richard's shoulder. "Don't you think?"

"Most days." Richard wanted to move away from the touch, but another part of him wanted to move closer, to take it in. Something else he needed to get under control. He couldn't be this starved for adult affection, could he? "I just knew I wanted to try to build my own legacy. I wanted to be able to point to my own ranch and say, 'I built that.'"

"Oh, hey. Yeah, I get it. I guess most men want that, don't they? In some form or another? I mean, maybe it's a company. Maybe it's a family. Whatever. We're programmed to want to leave our mark on the world, right?"

"I think so." Richard thought for a moment. "So if you sell your half of the land, what will you choose to build as a legacy?"

Joey blew out his breath, and Richard realized that the air between them was growing heavy. "I'm sorry, man. None of my business."

"Oh, no. It's not that. I just...I'm not sure, you know?" Joey cleared his throat. "Let's head back to the house."

"I'm sorry if I screwed up your hunting this morning."

"You didn't, all right? Stop apologizing. But they know we're in the vicinity now, so they won't show themselves again today. Not here, anyway. Maybe one of the other guys will have better luck."

Richard didn't answer. He still felt like this was all his fault.

"And if not," Joey continued with a quick grin, "We'll have already learned some important lessons from them, like where they den, and when they're active. Tomorrow we'll put that knowledge to good use, so bring plenty of ammo."

A gun sounded in the distance, echoing between the mountains sending a ripple of alarm through the air. Joey looked up. "Maybe one of my boys got lucky," he said with a laugh. "If so he owes us breakfast for scaring the coyotes his way. Come on, let's get out of here."

On the way down the mountain, Richard decided that his first foray into coyote hunting was a total disaster, regardless of what Joey said. He resolved to go home, do some deeper research, and be better prepared the next morning.

If there was a next morning. He really wouldn't blame Joey for asking him to step aside. But then there was the question of wiping out his savings to pay for Blueberry, and he didn't want to do that, either. Maybe Joey wouldn't ask, and Richard could do a better job of proving his worth the next day.

Chapter 10

Joey watched Richard go through the door in the kitchen, toward his office. He fought the urge to call him back, to apologize. What the hell had happened to him up there, anyway? Why had he gotten so nervous, when Richard was just enthusiastic about learning and ready to listen? And why had he nearly bolted when Richard started asking him about his family situation?

And it wasn't that he was prying, because he wasn't. Joey just didn't know, right now, how things were going to turn out, and that concerned him. He pulled his keys from his pocket and headed for the truck.

What was it Richard had asked him? What legacy would he build if Mack bought him out?

He didn't have an answer for that, and he hated it.

He'd always thought he would grow up, do this for a while, and then follow in his foster father's footsteps and become a disgruntled old farmer who barked at everyone and everything. It sounded like fun back then, and he had always imagined himself retiring there on the farm, where Cusp had raised him and Mack. Joey hadn't gotten the chance to pay back the man's kindness before he died, and that would probably eat at him for the rest of his life.

But if he sold to Mack, how else would he make the old man proud? How else would he show his gratitude? Joey didn't know, and for a moment he was irritated with Mack for making him decide.

But it wasn't really Mack's fault that he and his new wife had dreams, too, and they involved the land. Joey sure hadn't been around to help take care of the place. He'd spent plenty of money on it, sure, but he hadn't lived the day-to-day like Mack had. He hadn't ridden out the ups and downs. Mack deserved to own it.

But then what would Joey's future hold? All he'd ever known was that old farm and the man who left it to them. He'd always imagined himself as the same old man someday - just as grizzled, just as rigid, and just as good-hearted, when it counted. Hell, he'd been looking forward to never shaving again, and to grinning at people who thought he was just some dirt-poor illiterate, all the while he had six-figure bank accounts and more knowledge than most about farming and wildlife and cattle. He'd been excited to see what he and Mack could do with the place once they were in a financial position to really go whole hog.

He drove too fast, back toward the motel in town. It was nearly noon.

Cory waved at him when he walked by, a devilish smile on his face. Joey slowed and then stopped at the open office door. "Hey, what's up?" he asked.

Cory, still smiling, reached behind the desk and pulled out a brown-wrapped bottle. "You busy later? I get off early tonight."

Joey looked at the bottle Cory was waving around, then looked at Cory. He wanted to say yes. Hell, under almost any circumstances, he would say yes. Cory was probably a great guy, and Joey had no doubt that pickings were few and far between for a gay man in this town, but tonight he just wanted to be alone. He forced his smile wider. "Sorry, man. I've got a lot of paperwork to catch up on. Maybe another time."

Cory's smile faded. "OK," he said, putting the bottle back behind the desk. "No problem. Let me know if you change your mind."

Joey sighed. "No, seriously. I really have to get some work done. It's not about you, all right?"

He was lying. Ten seconds ago he hadn't been, but now that he thought Cory might be looking for more than a warm bed, he wasn't even going to go there. Joey Putnam didn't get attached, and he never would.

The thought of Richard - and his daughter - skittered through his mind, and he pushed it aside. "Catch you later," he said with a wave and walked toward his room, where he could lock the door and, hopefully, make a decision about Mack and the farm.

No, that wasn't right. It wasn't his place to make decisions about Mack. Mack was a grown man, even though Joey knew he would never really see him that way, and he was already making his own decisions. Joey's part just involved the farm. It was part of his dream, and he hated that he was possibly losing it, but Mack had a right to his dreams, too, and Mack and his wife were the one doing all the work. Joey realized he didn't even know her name.

That was a strange thought all its own. Mack? With a wife? The idea of it rolled around in Joey's head and wouldn't quite settle into a logical slot. In his mind, Mack was ten years old, getting the old man's farm truck stuck in the river. Or he was seven, following Joey and his friends everywhere they went. Sometimes he was sixteen, too, driving hard for a touchdown while Joey cheered him on. None of those things led Joey to the current knowledge that Mack was married and wanted to start a family.

And yet he was, and he did. Joey wasn't sure how he felt about that. He let himself into his room, poured a drink, and settled in to get some of next year's permit applications filled out, the TV on in the background.

He was deep into his third drink - Beam on ice - when a knock at the door brought his head up. He glanced toward the window and saw, to his surprise, that it was still light out. The guys had already texted him that they were done for the day, and that they were headed to the next town over for some food. He had declined the offer to go with them, because his mood just dictated that he brood by himself for a while. It happened every so often, and his crew knew it, and they got the hint.

So who was at the door?

He got up and walked across the ratty carpet to open it, intending to send whoever it was packing. Even Cory - the last thing he needed was a groupie, and the look on Cory's face earlier told him that was exactly what Cory wanted to be. So, no. Cory wasn't allowed inside. He reinforced this decision, one hand on the knob, then opened the door, intending to tell him to get lost.

Cory wasn't at the door.

Richard was.

"Oh." That was all Joey could think to say.

Richard had changed out of his heavier hunting gear. He was wearing cowboy boots, jeans and a blue button down that covered a white t-shirt. He smelled like horses and winter wind, and his hair was just messed up enough to make him look like he just rolled in from a walk on a beach somewhere. Even his tan looked good.

"Oh?" A smile played at Richard's lips.

"Um, yeah." Joey couldn't quite make his brain work. Instead, he opened the door a little farther and Richard came in and looked around.

"I'm not really in the mood for company," Joey said.

Richard finished taking stock of the room and glanced at him. Joey felt it. "Is that because of earlier?" Richard asked.

Earlier? Had something happened earlier?

"I didn't mean to make your job harder this morning."

Joey's shoulder relaxed. "I told you, man. You didn't. I've had way worse days in the woods. Trust me."

Richard sat in the chair Joey had just vacated and looked at the bottle. "You sure about that?" he asked, half grinning in a way that left a little wrinkle at the corner of his mouth. Joey wanted to lick it. Instead, he bit both lips.

Richard's grin faded a little. "Are you all right?" he asked.

Joey nodded. "What can I do for you man? I'm kinda..." He waved a hand toward the room in general, taking in the open suitcase on the only other chair, the TV, and the rumpled bed.

Richard nodded slowly. He put the bottle down and faced Joey full-on. "You want to be alone. I'm sorry. Is there anything I can do to help?"

"Nah." Joey was starting to feel the booze work, telling him to relax. Giving him the urge to talk.

"If this isn't about the hunt this morning, is it about your brother?" Richard asked.

Joey wanted to tell him to mind his own business and leave. On the other hand, he wanted Richard to stay...for less than noble reasons. He very carefully kept his eyes on Richard's face. His own body was heating up, and it wasn't just the drink. It was Richard, sitting in his room like he had a right to be here.

He stalked to the other chair, shoved the suitcase off it and sat down. "What can I do for you?" he asked, trying to keep his voice steady.

"Actually, Levi asked me to stop by on my way into town," Richard said. "For you." He pulled a white envelope from his pocket and handed it over. It would be a check, Joey knew, a very nice one. All for the nest egg that would...

What? Why was he worried about is nest egg? One more phone call and he wouldn't have a farm to build. Unless...

He looked at Richard, who was watching him closely. "How did you decide, about your farm?" he asked.

Richard blinked. "How did I...decide what?"

"How did you decide which place to buy?" Joey struggled to get the question out. "How did you choose where and how you wanted to live?"

Richard's smile came back. Good. "I took everything into account - Sasha, what she wanted, where she would be happiest growing up. I took into account what I wanted to do, too, and that was horses, the way Levi does it. Not that I'll ever hit that kind of success."

"You could."

Richard shook his head. "I don't even want it. Every day, Levi is involved in about a million things that need his attention. I can't afford that - Sasha gets all of my attention."

Joey remembered the little girl. "She's a cutie," he said. "Seems like a great kid."

"She is, and that's why I didn't blink when she wanted a farm closer to Comfort. Or wanted a horse of her own."

"So it's all about her?" Joey leaned forward and put his elbows on his knees, let his hands dangle between them.

"Every minute of every day. You said you don't have kids."

"Nope. Never wanted any. I'm too selfish for that."

"Oh, I don't know. I talked to Sasha, and she was pretty impressed with you. She wants me to invite you to supper - that's one reason I'm here, in fact." He leaned forward, closer to Joey's face. "I think she want to brag to her friends, to be honest."

Joey remembered his earlier thoughts about groupies and grinned to himself, but Richard caught it. "What?" he asked.

"Nothing. I was just thinking about being coyote famous," Joey answered, laughing.

"Well, the guy in the office - have you met him, kid named Cory? He thinks you two are an item."

Joey's jaw dropped. "Say again?"

"Don't worry," Richard said. "I won't tell a soul. I mean, you're both legal adults and everything, but I could see where a rumor like that could -."

"No. Nope. Not even." Joey raked a hand through his hair. He didn't know whether to be flattered that Cory was lying about them, or upset. He chose upset. "I knew he had a crush, but that's all it is, I swear."

Richard looked bemused. "Seriously, Joey. It's really none of my business."

But - and this thought slammed Joey hard - he wanted it to be Richard's business. He wanted to talk to Richard, who seemed suddenly like the best friend Joey never really had. He didn't know what to do about the farm, about Mack. Joey knew he worked best with a clear goal in mind, with a definite end point for all his hard work. But right now he found himself in the strange position of not knowing what to do next.

He didn't think too hard about it before taking a deep breath, scooping his coat off the back of the chair and saying, "Well, I can't deny a little princess her audience with the court jester," he said with a laugh. "So. What's for dinner?"

Chapter 11

Richard was nearly dumbfounded when Joey agreed to come over. Sasha had been adamant that he would, but Richard hadn't been so sure. He was fairly certain that Joey was a bit of a playboy, if Cory was to be believed, so he didn't actually think Joey would even be home, much less willing to spend an evening with a boring guy and a kid.

But here they were, Joey in Richard's passenger seat. Richard hadn't considered that Joey was drinking and couldn't drive, but that was all right. He didn't seem drunk, just a little...down. Richard would have to bring him back into town later.

His house was just on the other side of town and they were halfway there when Joey said, "Where is Sasha, anyway?"

Richard laughed. "She's in the backseat. You can't see her?"

Joey shot him a perplexed look. He twisted around, then after a minute he sank back down and glared at Richard. "She is not."

"How many of those drinks did you have before I saved you?" Richard was laughing and gripping the steering wheel too hard. The truck jogged across the center line and back.

"Not enough," Joey shot back. "Seriously, when you said that, I thought I was losing my mind for a second."

Richard just grinned and kept his eyes on the road. He wasn't sure what to expect when he walked up to Joey's motel room door with Levi's message, but it wasn't what he found - Joey all alone, apparently moping about...something.

OK, maybe moping was the wrong word. Maybe solitude was a better term, and the good Lord knew that Richard had wished for solitude a few times in his life, so he knew how it felt. He also knew that spending time with Sasha always made him feel better, and since he had promised her that he would invite Mr. Putnam to supper eventually, he did. It was impulsive, but Joey could have turned him down. In fact, Richard sort of expected him to.

Joey hadn't turned him down, though, and now Richard was letting him into the small house where he and Sasha ended their days with bedtime stories and silly jokes. "Make yourself at home," he said, gesturing toward the living room.

Joey stopped and looked around and Richard tried to imagine seeing the house through his eyes. The house was small, just a sort-of formal living room, an eat-in kitchen through the doorway behind Richard, a playroom for Sasha in the back, and two bedrooms upstairs. It wasn't much, especially compared to the airy open floor plan of Levi's big house, but it was cozy and it was plenty for him and Sasha. Neither of them much liked being in the house, anyway, not when there were horses to be ridden.

Instead of going to the sofa and sitting, Joey walked past Richard into the kitchen. He put a hand on the coffee pot, grabbed a cup from the hook above it, and poured himself a cup before sitting down at the round oak table. There was a cookie jar on the table. It was shaped like a duck. Only then did he look up to see Richard staring.

"What?" he asked. "You said make yourself at home."

"You're right, I did." Richard turned and walked to the bottom of the stairs. "Sasha? I'm back."

Joey was reaching for the cookie jar. Richard smacked his hand.

Joey pretended to pout.

"Hey - I'm treating you like home," he said. "Didn't your mother ever tell you no cookies before supper?"

Joey, to his surprise, nearly flinched.

Somehow, Richard had said something wrong. His gut twisted. "Hey, I'm sorry if that was out of line," he started, but Joey was already waving the comment away.

"No big deal. I don't like cookies anyway," he said, crossing his arms in a pout.

Richard chuckled, and Sasha chose that moment to come flying down the stairs, Pam right on her heels.

"Sasha, Pam. You two remember Joey, don't you?"

Sasha's face lit up and she scooted into a seat across from him. "You came!" she said to Joey.

"I did. Thanks for the invite." To Pam, he said, "We met a few evenings ago at the Broken Blue, right? Good to see you again."

Richard watched Joey's face, but whatever made him uncomfortable a moment ago was gone now. He sipped his coffee and sagged into the chair, completely at ease, it seemed. At least he wasn't drunk, as Richard had thought when he first opened the door at the motel and let him in. Richard had seen the bottle, but that wasn't what bothered him. It was the fact that Joey seemed so nonchalant about it. Nothing wrong with that, but it was still early and it made him wonder.

He wouldn't allow Sasha around drunks. Men who drank on occasion, sure - all the guys at the ranch had a beer or two now and then. But a drunk? No way.

But Joey had left the bottle behind without a second glance, and Richard figured he'd been worried for nothing.

"There's chili on the stove," Pam said, going to the back door and getting her coat off the hook. She'd just spent a good minute staring at Richard and then Joey, a secretive smile on her face, so her sudden words made Richard jump. Sasha laughed at that.

"Cornbread in the oven, too," Sasha announced, running to give Pam a hug. "See you tomorrow?"

Pam looked at Richard, who looked at Joey.

"What?" Joey asked.

"You want me to work tomorrow?" Richard asked, feeling slightly hesitant, not sure he wanted to know the answer.

Joey looked completely puzzled. "Why wouldn't you? I mean, didn't you tell Levi you would?"

"Sure." Richard turned a chair backward and straddled it. "But today..."

Joey waved a hand. "Today was a first day on new land. A lot of them go like that."

Richard wasn't sure he believed that, but he wasn't going to ask in front of Sasha. "If you're sure..."

"I'm sure." Joey sipped his coffee and met Richard's eyes over the rim of the cup. There was something unreadable there. Richard nodded and turned to Pam. "It'll be another early morning, if that's OK," he said.

"You know it's fine. Bring her in her jammies." She paused to tug at Sasha's hair and smile. "We'll make waffles."

"Yay!" Sasha bounced up and down in her chair. "Chocolate chip"

Pam pretended to look shocked. "Of course! There isn't any other kind, is there?"

"I had broccoli waffles once," Joey said. He'd been watching the exchange with a small smile. "They were totally delish."

"Eew! No!" Sasha looked so disgusted that Richard couldn't help but laugh.

"You sure?" Pam asked her. "You might like 'em. We could grind the broccoli up in the mixer and then..."

"No way." Sasha shook her head hard enough that her hair got into her eye. She swiped it away.

"Fine. We'll stick with chocolate, then." Pam waved and let herself out the door. "Bye. Y'all have fun."

"Let's eat!" Richard said, taking Sasha's hand and pulling her toward the other end of the kitchen, to the pot that was wafting steam on the stove. "Sasha, you get some plates and bowls."

He saw Joey starting to get up, but shook his head. Joey sat back down.

Richard grabbed the ladle and dipped out a bowl of chili for Joey. Then he cut a slice of cornbread from the pan and slathered the top with butter while Sasha watched. Putting it all on the plate, he handed it to Sasha. She was biting her lip in concentration. "Want to take this to our guest?" he asked.

She nodded and slowly walked that way, staring hard at the plate. They all breathed a sigh of relief when she made it, and Joey gave her a quick high-five. "Thank you. Did you help make it?"

She nodded, suddenly shy. "I cut up the peppers and mixed the cornbread with the mixer," she said. "It was easy."

"It is not easy!" Joey said. "I tried to mix cornbread once, but I just had one of those little mixers with the motor? Anyway, it was so loud that I got scared and dropped it while it was still going. It ran away, out the kitchen door. I never saw that mixer again," he finished sadly.

Sasha stared at him. Then, slowly, she giggled. "That's not true." She looked at Richard, then back to Joey. "Is it, Dad?"

"Well, I don't think Mr. Putnam would lie."

Once they were all settled at the table, Joey asked, "Sasha, did your dad tell me you liked to ride horses?"

"Yep," she mumbled around a bite of cornbread.

"Don't talk with your mouth full," Richard said.

"He did."

"It's true," Joey said. "I did."

He still was. Richard just rolled his eyes.

"Sasha is one of the best barrel racers in the county," Richard said.

"Can I show him my trophies?"

"After you eat, if he wants to see them."

"I won a trophy once," Joey said. "For growing the biggest watermelon."

Sasha looked at him, suspicious after the mixer story. "I didn't get to keep it, though. The government took it. Named it Venus." He shook his head. "I don't know where that thing went."

Richard and Sasha both groaned, which made Joey laugh.

He had a great laugh, Richard thought. The kind that was deep and resonant enough to make bystanders turn to see what was funny, but not so deep that he sounded like Santa Claus.

When he looked at Joey, Joey was looking back at him, a smile on his lips. "Thanks for feeding me," he said. "This is good."

Richard nodded. "Our pleasure. You two finish up and we'll go outside before it gets dark."

"Can Missy come over?" Sasha asked. Missy lived about a quarter mile down the road, and the two girls played together a lot. Richard started to say no, because they'd have such an early day tomorrow, but then he thought that wasn't Sasha's fault. It was his. "I guess, but only if her mother says it's OK."

She finished her chili, put her dishes in the sink, and tore out the back door.

"Wow, that's a lot of energy," Joey said, watching through the window behind the table. "I'm not sure I can get out of this chair, and she's halfway across the pasture."

Richard chuckled. "It never ends with that one." Then he got an idea and stood up. "Come on, if you're finished. Let's take them for a walk down by the river."

Joey groaned, but dragged himself out of the chair and helped Richard clear the table. Richard appreciated that, and he noticed a ghost of a smile on Joey's lips while they worked. "What?" he finally asked.

"This..." Joey waved toward the remains of supper. "Was nice. Thank you for inviting me."

"Oh. No problem. We don't really do fancy around here, but it fills the belly."

Joey laughed, making Richard smile. "I eat fast food three quarters of the time. This was a treat."

"Sasha would disagree, I think. She loves fast food, specifically chicken nuggets."

They pulled on their coats and Richard let them out onto the small patio at the side of the house. Farther on, in the yellow winter grass, they could see Sasha running, with another little girl right behind her. Richard raised his fingers to his lips and let out a whistle.

The girls waved and headed their way. Joey jumped. "You almost gave me a heart attack."

"It's all that fast food," Richard said.

"Very funny."

Sasha and Missy caught up with them. Each of them grabbed one of Richard's hands. "We're going for a walk. Want to come?" he asked.

"Will we be back before dark?" Missy asked. She was a quiet kid, more shy than fiery. She and Sasha were so different it was amazing that they could be friends.

"We will if you need to be," Richard said.

"Where are we going?" Sasha asked.

"The river."

With that, the girls ran ahead. "Have you seen any coyotes around this part of the county?" Joey asked, watching them go.

"No." Richard frowned at the small spike of fear that shot down his spine. "Of course, I haven't been looking too closely."

"We'll look now," Joey said. "If they're around, there'll be evidence at the river."

Richard didn't like the idea of keeping Sasha - or Missy, for that matter - cooped up inside, but he hadn't really considered the coyotes roaming this far south. His house was a good four miles over land from the Broken Blue.

"Oh, they'll travel this far for the right food," Joey said when he mentioned it. "But the odds are, they haven't. We know where their den is now, and they don't like getting too far away. Besides, they mostly hunt at night. You don't let the girls out here in the dark, do you?"

Richard said, "Not unsupervised. They like to play out late in the summer, though. Fireflies."

"Well, that just means we'll have to work hard to thin down this herd, huh?"

That was exactly what it meant, and Richard was thankful to Joey for pointing it out. He knew, in the back of his head, that the danger was there, but he hadn't taken it too seriously. "Don't they only come after humans when they're starving?" he asked.

Joey nodded. "Yep. Mostly. But no animal will turn down an easy meal." He nodded. "These two are loud, but they're still pretty small, compared to a coyote."

Richard nodded. "I guess I should be paying more attention."

"Like I said," Joey answered, putting a hand on his arm, "If you haven't seen them out here in the winter, when food is scarce, they probably haven't roamed this far from the den yet. We'll take care of them before they can."

The river was flowing fast, splashing against the rocky bank. Sasha and Missy were playing nearby, but keeping a safe distance. "Hey, Sasha," Joey called.

Both girls ran over.

"You need to teach Missy what you learned about the coyotes," he said, "and then both of you look for signs of them here on the bank, all right?"

Sasha grinned. "Ooh, yeah. That'll be fun."

"See what you can find, then show us, all right?"

Both men watched the two of them run off, Sasha chattering as they went. "That was a good idea," Richard said. "If they're going to be playing out here, they need to know. Both of them."

"Also, Sash will learn better if she teaches someone else."

"True." Richard paused. "Listen, Joey. About earlier...if I said something wrong, I didn't mean to, you know?"

Beside him, Joey smiled. "You didn't, not really. It was just a reaction."

"To the cookies, or to the crack I made about your mom? I really didn't mean anything." Richard had been wondering what had triggered Joey's response, but he hadn't had time to ask till now. "Do you not get along with your mom?" he asked.

Joey was quiet for a few steps. Then he said, "I don't know. I never knew her."

"Oh. Sorry."

Maybe he was adopted, or maybe she died during childbirth. Richard already felt like he'd overstepped, and he didn't want to push his luck.

But then Joey started talking, his voice low but steady. "She and my dad apparently had some issues. Drugs, maybe some abuse, I don't know for sure. It's all just rumors around the little town where I grew up. Anyway, they took off or something when I was four and my brother Mack was just one."

"They..." Richard swallowed the sudden lump in his throat. "You mean they just left you somewhere?"

"Apparently. We were almost dead when our neighbor, Cusp, found us. He's the old guy who owned the next farm over. He and my dad supposedly had some kind of share in some equipment, and when my dad didn't show up one day, he came looking."

"That's pretty lucky for you," Richard said, trying not to imagine the little boy Joey had been, scared and hungry. It was too heart-breaking to think about.

Joey chuckled. "I think Cusp was madder about his tractor than being saddled with two kids."

Richard frowned. "He...he just kept you?"

Joey shrugged. "No one else wanted two more mouths to feed, and he couldn't just leave us there to die." He must have noticed the surprised look on Richard's face. "No, he went through all the proper channels and officially adopted us, more or less. He didn't just kidnap us or anything. They never found my parents, either, so he raised us."

"Wow. I can't imagine just...leaving Sasha behind." Richard kicked at a clump of dead grass and looked out across the darkening field at his little girl. He suddenly wanted her beside him, holding his hand. "That's pretty crazy, Joey."

"I didn't choose them, it was just the luck of the draw," Joey answered with a chuckle. Richard thought that chuckle was a rueful sound. "In any case, Cusp did a good job, considering what he had to put up with, I guess."

Richard smiled at that. He didn't have a little boy, but he'd been one, and that was enough to give him a pretty clear picture - an old man, two rough and tumble kids. "I bet you kept him busy," he said.

"We did. I learned a lot from him, though."

"I bet he'd be proud of you now."

Joey glanced up from his steps. "Do you do that all the time?"

Richard didn't know what he was talking about. "What?"

"See the brighter side of things? You always come up with a rosy side."

"Do I do that?" Richard thought about Sasha again, and how he'd always determined to make life a positive experience for her. "I guess I do, but I have a good reason."

Joey waited, thankfully, while he got his thoughts in order. "When Sasha's mother took off, it devastated her. She was just at that age, you know? Where she wasn't old enough to understand but she was old enough to be super attached. All she wanted was her mommy, and it was the one thing I couldn't give her."

"What did you do?"

It occurred to Richard that there were similarities between Sasha's story and Joey's. "Honestly, I yelled for help, as loud and as fast as I could."

Joey laughed and Richard smiled. "I didn't know much about taking care of a baby. All that stuff you hear about how you'll instinctively know what to do? Nope - that's a lie. I was lost. I mean, I knew she need to be clean, to be fed, to be held, but that was about it. I was exhausted and scared."

"So? Did you get the help you yelled for?" Joey asked. There was a ring of real interest in his voice. He wasn't just being polite.

"I did. Pam came running. Levi and his sister did, too. Cruz wasn't around yet, but nearly everyone else associated with the Broken Blue had a hand in keeping Sasha alive and healthy." It had been a rough year, that first one. Alone with a baby that he couldn't communicate with, but loved more than life itself, he remembered the dread he felt whenever he looked at her. Because he knew, somehow, he was going to mess up. He was going to hurt her, or scare her, or something. Because he had no idea what he was doing. Tiny fists, bright eyes, a cry that cut him to the bone. He shook his head, remembering.

"But you figured it out," Joey prompted.

"I figured it out. Carol, Levi's sister, taught me how to bathe her properly. Pam taught me how to keep her clean, and how to feed her. She also taught me to understand all the different cries - when she was hungry, when she was cold, whatever."

"Wait - babies have different cries?" Joey looked impressed.

"Yep. But man, the hardest thing is figuring out which is which. The poor kid only knew, like twenty words, and when she was really wound up she couldn't get any of them out. I mean, you learn eventually, but it takes time to figure out that the tired cry is quieter than the hungry cry, or that the hungry cry is slower than the 'I just got bit by a bug' cry. It's terrifying."

Joey started laughing.

"What?"

"I'm just imagining you running around crazy, trying to explain things to a little baby."

"Well, then you'll think it's extra funny when you realize that she was old enough to toddle around, so half my life was trying to keep her from falling off edges. The porch, the bathtub, the hay loft...it was insanity."

"You let her into the hay loft?" Joey asked, half grinning.

"I had to, for a while. I couldn't leave her home alone while I went to work. Once Pam's kids got older, she started watching Sasha for me, but before that I was on my own a lot."

"I'm sorry, man. That had to be tough."

"It was the toughest, best thing that ever happened to me. She was the ranch mascot for a while, and all the guys helped me take care of her." He laughed at the memory. "You want to know what really saved me, though?"

"What?"

"Horses. Sasha grew up riding with me, at the ranch. She was on horseback almost as much as I was in those days. And she loved it, started asking for her own horse at three. She learned to ride on her own at four, and she was barrel racing that same year."

"Wow."

"Tell me about it." Richard looked over at his daughter and smiled.

Chapter 12

Joey took in Richard's story, comparing it to his own. In the back of his mind, he was also amazed at how comfortable he was here. When he first accepted the invitation, he was sure he'd be in for a somewhat awkward evening - he still barely knew Richard. But the alternative was drinking himself into a stupor in his ugly-ass motel room, and he didn't want to do that, either.

So he had come, and he was honestly enjoying himself. He'd been out with plenty of guys, but Richard was somehow different. Maybe it was the little girl, Sasha, or maybe it was the quiet setting, but something sure was nice.

They were sitting on the rocky riverbank, watching the sun disappear behind the mountains. The kids were playing nearby, building what looked a little like a sandcastle but more like a giant anthill. The sand wasn't wet enough for them, and every time part of the structure collapsed they groaned.

"Are all of your evenings this nice?" Joey asked, leaning back on the big slab of cold limestone and looking at his breath in the air. He felt the last of the sun's warmth held within the stone and let his fingers slide over the rough edges.

Richard nodded. "Usually. Once in a while things get out of control, especially in the summer." He frowned. "And the winter. Unless there is some school thing going on, or it's rodeo season, we're hanging out either here or at the Broken Blue. I try not to do that too much, because they spoil Sasha silly."

"So I heard." Joey wanted to know more. He wanted to understand a lot more about Richard and how he managed to raise a child on his own. What kind of man did that? What kind of man was brave enough to do that?

He considered himself brave enough, if that was the word, but he was nothing compared to men like Richard and Cusp, who voluntary took responsibility for fragile lives. Hell, half his work was taking lives, not protecting them.

And suddenly that didn't sit right with him. Not that he was going to quit his work or anything. He knew he performed a needed, healthy service to man and beast, but now, talking with Richard and hearing the quiet, content resolve in his voice, he thought maybe it wouldn't be too bad to give back to life a little too. He leaned back on his elbows, rolling that around in his head. It felt right, the idea of it, anyway. One of Cusp's famous pieces of advice popped into his head.

Find a way to give back as much as you take, son. That way you pay your debts.

Joey had known, even then, that he wasn't talking about monetary debts but something deeper and more important. But how did he give back? What did he give back? He didn't have kids to raise, or even his brother to support, now that Mack had gone and gotten married. He didn't have anything, really.

The thought brought him up short. He didn't have anything. He didn't have anybody, either.

Sure, his crew was there - all of them were friends. And he could always find some company when he wanted it, if he wanted it. But with Mack on the farm, and with Joey's constant traveling, he really didn't have a lot of time or opportunity to put down roots of his own.

He saw his days sliding by, in his mind, a lot like the river near his dangling feet. He saw how the threads that tied those hours and days together was thin, easily broken.

But he had his freedom, didn't he? And that was something, wasn't it?

"Hey. You all right?" Richard was looking at him, his forehead wrinkled up in curiosity. "You kind of got lost there for a minute."

"Yeah, I do that. Just thinking about work," Joey said. He fiddled with one of the brass buttons on his jacket. It was cold. "I kind of zoned out there for a minute. This place does that to you, doesn't it?"

Richard nodded and laughed. "It does, if you take the time to let it."

He turned back around and watched the kids, still playing. Joey glanced that way, too. Now they were tossing rocks into the river, competing to make the biggest splash.

But his eyes were drawn back to Richard. Richard had the kind of look on his face that every parent should have when they were looking at their child, Joey thought. A mix of pride and happiness and weight, knowing how important it was to do this one job right. And Richard seemed to be doing it right.

He was about to call to Sasha, and ask her if she found any coyote tracks, when a horn blew from somewhere back toward the house, long and deep. All four of them jumped. Joey turned to see headlights in the gloom, coming down the driveway. It wasn't a normal car, though - too much rattling. It sounded like a pickup hauling a trailer. Beside him, Richard muttered, "What the hell is he doing?"

They walked back toward the house, Sasha and Missy running ahead. "Missy?" Richard called. "It's about time for you to head home."

Missy and Sasha groaned, but when they got to the fence, Missy headed off in the other direction. Now that it was just about dark, Joey could see lights on in a house farther on. Good - that meant Missy wouldn't be out by herself for long. Sasha ran back to her daddy and grabbed his hand.

"What is Uncle Levi doing?" she asked, looking up at him.

"I have no idea, sweetheart. Let's go see."

Levi and Cruz greeted them when they got to the house, not saying much but grinning hard. It was Levi's truck - Joey recognized it now - and it was pulling a long silver horse trailer. Sasha eyed it carefully but stayed by Richard's side.

"We wanted to get here earlier, but there was a small emergency at the ranch," Cruz said, leaning against the fender of the truck and folding his arms.

Richard frowned. "Everything all right?"

Levi chuckled. "Yeah. Sonny almost burnt down the foreman's house trying to make a pot roast."

Richard's face cleared and he laughed. "Sonny is trying to learn to cook," he explained to Joey. "He and Deacon - that's Levi's ranch foreman - are getting married in a couple of months, and he wants to make the feast himself."

"Well, at least he's willing to learn," Cruz said.

"True. A lot of men wouldn't."

A soft whinny came from inside the trailer.

Levi smiled.

Richard frowned.

Sasha gasped and took off running in that direction.

"Blueberry?" Richard asked, his voice low.

Levi nodded. "Blueberry. No need for her to wait."

Richard shot him a look that, to Joey, held a lot of anger, and followed Sasha.

Levi looked at Joey and shrugged. "He'll be mad for a minute, but he'll get over it."

Then he and Cruz turned away and went to help them unload the horse. Joey followed along behind them, thinking that he couldn't imagine Richard really mad. When he got there, Sasha was begging her daddy for a ride.

"Honey, it's too dark. You don't want Blueberry to get hurt, do you?" Richard asked, kneeling down in front of her.

She pointed toward the cab of the truck, a pout on her face. "What if I stay in the headlights?" she asked, barely managing to keep from jumping up and down. Her little body shook all over, like an excited puppy.

"I think we should wait until tomorrow." He reached for her, but she pulled away and ran to the speckled bay appaloosa and hugged its shoulder.

Richard turned to Levi. "I may have to kill you," he said over the sound of her soft crying.

Levi shrugged and grinned. "Let her ride. Go get your truck, give her some light."

"It's almost seven - her bath time," Richard argued, but Joey could see him giving in, slowly, as his eyes slid back to his daughter.

Joey walked away for a moment and pulled out his phone. One of his men, Clay, answered. "You boys sober?" Joey asked.

"Yeah, boss. Early morning tomorrow."

"All right. Grab my truck keys, and bring every truck we've got out here to Richard's ranch."

"All of them? What for?"

"We need 'em." He gave Clay quick directions and hung up, just in time to hear Cruz say, "She could just skip school tomorrow. It's going to snow anyway."

"No, she can't," Richard said.

"I used to do it all the time."

"Cruz..."

Cruz laughed and slung an arm around Levi. "I know, I know...that's how I turned into such a heathen."

"I'm about to solve this problem," Joey said. The three other men turned to look at him. It occurred to him briefly that he might be overstepping his bounds here, but he shrugged it off. If nothing else, Richard could be mad at him instead of at his boss.

"What are you doing?" Richard asked.

"Give me five minutes," Joey answered.

Sasha wasn't crying anymore, but she wasn't letting go of Blueberry, either. The horse stood firm and let her hang onto him. Joey walked over to her and knelt down carefully. He wasn't afraid of horses, but he knew to be careful around them, too. Sasha stared at him, her face streaked and dirty from playing in the sand earlier.

"You want to ride tonight?" he asked.

"Yes," she whispered, her gaze sliding past him to her father.

"If I can make that happen, will you promise to get your bath and go right to bed afterward?"

She sniffed and wiped her nose on the horse, then she nodded. "Promise."

"Good enough." Joey stood up in time to see more head-lights cut through the darkness at the end of the driveway.

He and his crew, altogether, had four trucks with them on this job, and now they were making their way down the short driveway. Not looking at Richard, he jogged over to meet them and direct them to park in the field behind the house, explaining what he wanted.

Richard was staring at him in amazement. Levi laughed out loud, throwing his head back, and Cruz jumped into the truck to join the circle behind the house. By the time all the trucks were parked, headlights on, the whole field was lit up like a football stadium and his guys were cheering for Sasha to ride. Joey laughed as Levi walked past them and Richard helped Sasha mount the horse bareback.

She *tsk*ed at the horse and he headed for the lights and noise without any hesitation, leaving Richard standing beside Joey in the near dark. Richard said, "You are going to spoil her as badly as they do." He nodded toward Levi's retreating back.

"Aww, come on. You used to be a kid, you remember wanting something so bad. This is fun." Joey pointed. "And my guys were bored anyway, so they needed something to do."

Richard shook his head. "You talk about them like they're kids, too."

"Well, if they get bored enough, they sort morph into little troublemakers. I'm killing two birds with one horse here." As he talked he watched Richard's face. His features looked sharp in the light from the field.

Joey relaxed when he saw that Richard was exasperated at the bunch of them, but not really mad. Joey reached and put a hand on his arm. "It's fun, it's fine. Trust me. This will be a much fonder memory than just another bedtime."

He was suddenly aware of how close Richard was standing. On impulse, he leaned in and kissed Richard, who gasped a little. But he didn't pull away. Joey tasted him, the chili, the sweetness, and then he let go and turned back toward the lights. "Come on," he said. "You're missing it."

Richard had the back of his hand against his lips, blinking at Joey, but he followed. Up ahead, Sasha was laughing and showing off for his guys, putting Blueberry through his paces. Her laughter filled the darkness and Joey thought it was the nicest sound he'd ever heard.

He walked up to one of the trucks and stood beside Cruz. "I saw that," Cruz said. "What's going on?"

"Damned if I know, but I like it," Joey said, still watching the girl and her horse. He wasn't lying - he didn't know what had made him kiss Richard - but he was surprised by just how strongly he wanted to do it again.

Chapter 13

Richard felt like he'd been punched, not kissed. He watched Joey walk ahead, sauntering over to Levi to talk, as if what had just happened was no big deal. Well, it sure as hell felt like a big deal. He glanced to see if Sasha had noticed, but she was in her element on Blueberry's back. The two of them had a special chemistry and half the time, in the arena, they looked like they might be dance partners instead of horse and rider.

Speaking of chemistry…He licked his lips, still tasting chili spice and a hint of whiskey from Joey's lips. Richard fought the urge to catch up with him, pull him back into the shadows for another kiss. For more, maybe.

Then he shook his head, wondered what the hell was going on with him, and walked toward the makeshift ring to cheer for his daughter. In spite of the cold, he was burning up and trembling like he had a fever.

Maybe I do, he thought. He knew that Sasha kept him so busy that he didn't take proper care of himself. He didn't date, and he had no desire for a one night stand.

And the odds were, that was what Joey wanted. Richard had seen enough of his kind at the ranch – guys skating into town for work and then skating back out again, often finding a little temporary shelter with another worker or one of the locals to keep them company. Then they'd be gone, off to the next town, the next job, maybe never coming back.

Richard didn't care what people did, but he didn't want to bring even a hint of that into Sasha's life. He'd rather just be alone, no matter how much he wanted more of Joey's kiss. No matter how curious he was about the man. No matter what. Sasha was his life, and there was no room for casual hookups. Joey might be used to this sort of thing, but Richard didn't have to be part of it.

Still, he couldn't help imagining what Joey might feel like beside him in bed, curled up against the cold winter nights.

Shaking off his thoughts, he cheered for her along with all the others, letting her have her fun for the next hour. In the midst of it all, he kept catching Joey's eye. No matter when he looked, Joey seemed to be looking back at him, and in spite of the cold there was definitely heat in that gaze, and heat between the two of them. He nailed his gaze to Sasha and kept it there.

By the time he talked her off the horse, the guys were starting to leave. She was flushed and laughing with excitement, and he directed her to go thank every one of those guys for letting her ride tonight. She did, without a moment's hesitation. He watched her go to each one, shoulders back and head high, and shake their hand. Except for Levi, of course - he picked her up and swung her around like a toy, making her squeal. Richard couldn't help but be proud of her.

After the men had gone, including Levi and Cruz and the check he insisted they take, he got Sasha calmed down enough to get her into bed. "Blueberry was a good surprise," she said sleepily, grabbing his hand and giving it a hug. "Thank you, Daddy."

He bent down to kiss her forehead. "Don't thank me - this was Uncle Levi's idea. You've got a lot of responsibility now, you know. The guys won't be around to take care of Blueberry, so you have to do all of it."

She nodded. "I know. You'll teach me, right?"

He smiled. "I will, but you know most of it. Anyway, you need to listen to me - this means you have to be here to take care of him. No more sleepovers, no summer camp. And he'll be lonely here, away from all the other horses, so you've got to spend time with him every day."

He knew she would - Blueberry really was her best friend. Still, he wanted to make sure she knew how important it was that she take good care of him. Somewhere in the back of his mind, he worried that she would grow out of her horse fascination, and Richard would end up taking care of the animal. Maybe he was just worried for nothing, though. He hoped so.

"Can I ride him over to the Broken Blue to visit sometimes?" she asked. "So he can see his friends?"

"Uhh, we'll see." The ranch was miles away, even through the woods. That would be too dangerous for her alone. "Maybe if I come with you."

"Mmkay," she said.

"You want a story?"

She was already asleep. He kissed her on the forehead and turned out her light.

His phone rang as he walked back through the kitchen on his way to the patio out back. He needed to do some serious thinking, and he always did that best outside.

It was Joey, maybe the last person Richard wanted to talk to right now.

"What's up?" he asked, trying to keep his voice steady. He knew what was up. He knew Joey would probably want to come back tonight, maybe finish what he started. He wouldn't understand keeping this stuff away from Sasha, or respecting Richard's more important obli-.

"Did Sasha have fun tonight?" Joey asked. His voice was sleepy and slow.

"She had a blast. Thanks for making it happen."

"The guys had fun, too. They want to host a cookout this weekend," Joey said. "At your place, I mean. If that's OK."

"Um, sure, I guess. Why here, though?"

"I don't know, it was their idea. I just told them I'd ask." He paused. "You don't have to do anything. We'll bring the food, if you can point us toward wood for a bonfire. Invite the guys at the Broken Blue, too, or I will."

"That...sounds like a lot of fun. It's a good idea, and Sasha will love it. Thanks." Then something occurred to him. "Joey, your guys won't raise too much hell, will they? I need Sasha to be safe."

There was a pause, and Joey said, "They'll be fine." His voice was suddenly awake, his tone clipped.

"Oh, I'm sure they will, just, you know..." Richard cringed. He was pretty sure he had just pissed Joey off, but oh well. Better that than bring a rowdy party around Sasha. "Whatever you think."

He hung up, sure that tomorrow Joey would call the whole thing off. Maybe Joey didn't understand because he didn't have kids, but Richard would do nothing that might even hint at impropriety, not where Sasha was concerned. That included drunks, drugs, or anything else.

Still, if Joey could keep his guys - and himself - under control, it sounded like fun, and Richard went to bed thinking that a party might be just the change of pace he needed to kick off a busy spring and summer.

Three the next morning came early, and he carried Sasha to Pam's house in her pajamas, her school clothes in a bag for later. Once he got her settled, he said goodbye, telling Pam that if Sasha really was too tired for school, she had his permission to keep her at home.

Still rubbing his own eyes and fighting back a few yawns, he put the truck in gear and pointed it toward the ranch.

Joey didn't even look at him when he got out of the truck and came over to say hello. He was looking at the map again. Richard greeted the other men and hoisted his rifle further onto his shoulder and stood there, waiting to move out.

Joey finally turned and held up the map, still not looking at Richard. "OK, we've had sightings here, here, and here," he said, pointing. It's late in the year, and smack in the middle of mating season, so they'll be hunting hard these next couple of weeks. They're running out of food, most likely. You guys want the same arrangement as before?"

The men mumbled their assent and signed off on the map.

Joey finally looked at Richard, but his eyes were hard. "You ready?"

Richard nodded and followed along behind Joey, feeling like there was definitely something wrong. He just couldn't figure out what, and he didn't think now was the time to ask. Joey kept up a quick pace until they were halfway up the trail from the day before, and then he pointed. "I'm going out here. I need you watching the south corner of this clearing. I'll stay west. Just keep my general direction in mind and try not to shoot me, all right?"

"Sure," Richard said.

Joey looked at him for a moment, and the tension hung in the air between them. Finally he tossed Richard the extra radio he was carrying and turned away. "I'll use my calls to draw them into the clearing, if I can. Be ready. Yell if you get in trouble." He nodded toward the radio. "It's already set to our frequency."

"All right." Richard watched him stalk through the trees and disappear into the darkness. Then he sighed, shook his head, and made his way down the trail to his assigned spot. As quietly as he could, he settled himself against a thick tree with low-hanging branches and waited.

Chapter 14

Joey was so pissed off he didn't even want to look at Richard this morning. He thought about sending him back home, but that would leave him without a partner, and he didn't lightly break his own rules. That didn't mean he had to talk to the man, though. Being near him was enough to piss Joey off all over again.

But once he was seated comfortably in the hollow they had used the day before, he couldn't get Richard out of his head. He kept replaying the man's words from the night before, feeling the sting of them every time he remembered. *Your guys won't raise too much hell, will they? I need Sasha to be safe.* He'd sounded so smug, so parental.

As if Joey would do anything to put a child in jeopardy. As if he would disrespect Richard like that. He shook his head, but the words came back again. He was half tempted to call the whole thing off, but that would require explaining things to his crew, and he didn't want to do that, either. It wasn't their fault that Richard was, apparently, an uptight asshole. It was true that these men could get rowdy, and they liked to drink and raise hell. Joey wasn't denying that at all. But they also knew when to straighten up and fly right. They knew how to act when kids were present.

Hell, he even understood that Richard didn't know them that well, so he would naturally have concerns, but surely he had seen that everyone was on good behavior the night before, and he could assume that they would be again this weekend. He *could* assume that, but obviously he didn't.

Joey knew he was fuming, but he couldn't pull himself out of the thought loop that was making him madder and madder. He watched for any sign of coyote, hoping one would show up just so he could refocus. He cycled through several calls and waited, then did it again. He glanced around, but couldn't see Richard from where he was sitting. That was probably for the best, because right now he didn't want to talk to him.

And why the hell had he kissed the man last night? What had gotten into his head that he would try something like that? Technically, he could almost consider Richard his employer.

But Richard had looked so damned happy. Joey hadn't been able to take his eyes off the man's lips, curved into a soft smile as he watched his daughter in the glow of the headlights. It was the kind of look that every dad should give his kid - proud, loving, and something else, something Joey couldn't quite name. Watching, he'd been sucked into Richard and Sasha's little world for a moment. And then he'd let his feelings get a little bit out of control. And then they were kissing, and Joey was tasting the tang of Richard's lips. He damned near melted inside.

And then he realized what he was doing and left before things could get any worse.

His phone vibrated silently in his pocket, dragging his attention back to the early morning woods. Carefully, he pulled it out and saw a message from Mack light up the screen.

You sober? Along with a smiley face.

Of course he was sober. It was...he checked the screen again...four fifteen in the morning.

What? he typed, dimming the screen. He wouldn't answer at all, but it might be important.

You were supposed to call me back.

Oh, yeah. He'd forgotten to do that. Then again, he thought, maybe he hadn't forgotten. It sure as hell felt like he'd just been putting it off, now that he thought about it. *Will call when I'm out of the woods today. Around noon?*

Another smiley face. He guessed that was a yes and put the phone away.

The cold morning air bit at his cheeks. He put one hand over his mouth and tried to breathe warmer air over his face, but it didn't work very well. The morning was still dark and really quiet, more quiet than woods usually were this time of the morning. That worked out well when, about ten minutes later, he heard the unmistakable sound of an animal moving toward the clearing.

He set up and aimed his rifle in the general direction of the sound, slowing his breath and scanning the shadows between the trees. He didn't have to wait long - a coyote stuck her muzzle out into the clearing. She was just sniffing around, checking it out. It might have been the same female from yesterday, but he couldn't be sure.

Eventually she stepped out of the trees, making a nice target from Joey's vantage point. Through the scope, he could see other movement behind her - other members of her pack, staying close.

They would scatter when he took the shot, there was no way around it. He could only hope that they would scatter in the direction of his guys, on the other segments of the property.

He took a long breath and squeezed the trigger. The shot was loud in the quiet cold, the gun hot in his hands. The coyote dropped. A clean shot. As expected, the others scattered.

No more than a second later, he heard another shot close by. Another yelp. That would be Richard. Two kills this morning would be fantastic. And if one of the other guys managed to put one down, that would make for a damned productive morning.

And that's why I'm here, he thought, pulling the young female off the path. That's the only reason I'm here. To cull this pack. Not to kiss the cowboys, not to fall for the help, but to...

His thoughts stopped short.

Whoa. Nope.

Hold on.

He wasn't falling for anyone. He wasn't interested in anything serious. That wasn't who he was, and it wasn't what he wanted.

Was it?

No. It wasn't. He wasn't that kind of guy. He was more...well...

He dropped the coyote at the edge of the path and just stood there, looking into the darkness. What kind of guy was he?

More importantly, what kind of guy did he want to be?

This was a stupid line of thought. He had work to do.

The coyote was a clean shot, right through her lung. He stood up straight and let out a low whistle, a lot like the one Richard had used the night before to get Sasha's attention. He smiled at the thought of how he'd startled at the sound.

Richard came into sight after a couple of minutes, pulling his own coyote - an older male, with gray around its muzzle - along the path behind him. Joey looked away from him, but that felt too hateful, so he looked back and forced a smile.

Richard was beaming, but there was something else behind his eyes. He searched Joey's face when he got close enough, his brow wrinkled, and then forced a smile of his own. "Got one," he said.

Joey nodded. "We've got to go get an ATV and a trailer. I think one of my other guys might have shot one, too."

"I heard that. I'll go get the trailer."

Joey watched him go, relieved that he didn't have to stand and chat. He pulled out his radio and keyed in to the others. "Anybody get a kill?" he asked.

The radio crackled in his hand. Steve. "Looks like Price has one. We dragging them out?"

"No," Joey replied, fully aware that Richard would be able to hear them talking with his own set. "Richard's going to get a four-wheeler. Just sit tight."

"Aww," Steve said. "Did he give you a goodbye kiss?"

Joey's face went hot. "Shut the hell up," he snapped.

The radio went silent, but the damage was already done. Steve must have seen what happened last night, and now he was giving Joey hell for it. Normally that wouldn't be a problem, but normally the object of Joey's kisses wasn't listening in, either.

Maybe he had his radio off. It had been off when Joey gave it to him, so maybe Richard simply hadn't turned it on.

Twenty minutes later, with the sound of the ATV engine cutting through the quiet morning, Richard shot Joey a look that told Joey he had heard, and it wasn't funny.

Joey took a deep breath. He didn't look at Richard while they silently loaded the animals onto the trailer, and he didn't look at him when they picked up the other coyote and headed off the mountain. He was behind Richard in the seat, keeping an eye on the trailer. He could feel the tension in Richard's body.

Well, it was probably for the best. Richard thought he was dangerous to be around Sasha anyway, right? And he thought Richard was too uptight to have any real fun. The attraction was just a passing physical thing, and that was no big deal.

Levi was waiting for them when they got to the bottom of the hill, and helped them load the coyotes into the bed of Joey's truck. He already had a local tanner lined up for these pelts, so all he had to do was drop them off.

They worked in near silence until the truck was loaded. Levi stood up and said to Richard, "Everything all right?"

Richard shot a glance at Joey. "Sure," he said.

Levi looked at Joey next, his eyebrows raised. Joey just shrugged and went around to start the truck before Levi could ask him the same question.

No, everything wasn't all right. Levi could probably feel the tension in the air between Richard and Joey, but Joey wasn't about to try to explain it. Apparently, Richard wasn't either.

But what was there to explain, anyway? They had managed to piss each other off, and that was that. Another two or three mornings like this one and Joey and his crew would be gone by the end of the week, so it wouldn't matter. Joey slammed the door too hard and turned back toward Levi, just as his men came walking down the farm road, talking among themselves.

Good, some interference. He needed that right now. He was very careful not to look at Richard while he signed off on the small receipt that acted as a log for his kills on this land. Steve shot him a sheepish look, but then shrugged and put his rifle in the truck.

When he was sure all of the guys were off the mountain and headed back to the motel, he pulled out in his own truck, only relaxing when he was through the Broken Blue's main gate and on the highway back to town. Later he would talk to the guys about this weekend, maybe try to talk them out of it, or talk them into moving it to the Broken Blue. Whatever they did, he didn't want to spend any more time around Richard than he had to. It was just too damned confusing, and he didn't like Richard's attitude.

Chapter 15

Richard didn't take a deep breath until he was back in his office, alone. Between Joey being all pissed off and Levi looking at him like he was keeping secrets, he really would have liked to hide out for the rest of the day.

Of course that wasn't going to happen, though. In less than an hour he was hemmed in by Levi and Cruz, trapped behind his desk with no hope of escape until they finished drilling him for information.

Cruz was sitting on the corner of the desk, staring down at him. "Levi said there were issues this morning."

Richard wondered if playing dumb would work. "What issues?"

"Well that's the question, isn't it?" Cruz said.

"What was up with you two?" Levi was frowning at Cruz, but then he frowned at Richard, too. "Everything seemed fine last night, but then this morning I figured one of you wasn't coming out of the woods alive."

"I don't know what you mean..." Richard shifted his gaze toward some paperwork, hoping they would think he was busy and leave him alone.

Cruz huffed. "Oh, come on. You were kissing last night -.

Richard looked up sharply.

Cruz leaned in and raised an eyebrow. "Yeah, I saw that. And today, you hate each other's guts? That doesn't happen just because, Richard."

Richard rubbed his hands over his face. "Listen guys, I don't know what happened last night. Yes, he kissed me, but I didn't ask for it and I didn't expect it."

Cruz grinned. "Well, you sure as hell looked like you were enjoying it."

Richard groaned. "Well, whatever happened, it doesn't matter. By the way, I was told to invite everybody to a shindig at my place this weekend."

That worked. Cruz couldn't turn down a party. "I'll make potato salad, and maybe some of those little rolls you like." He stopped at looked at Richard. "Who's planning this party?"

Richard shrugged. "I guess Joey's guys. It was their idea."

Cruz shook his head and pursed his lips. "They're gonna need help. I'll call him now."

Then he was gone, leaving Richard staring and Levi grinning. "You did that on purpose," Levi said.

"Yeah, but it's true."

Levi sat, taking Cruz's spot on the corner of Richard's desk. "Well, you don't sound happy about it."

Richard sighed. He didn't want to go into it, mostly because he wasn't sure what 'it' was in the first place. "I'm just worried they'll get out of hand around Sasha, I think."

"They won't. We'll be there."

"You're right. Joey won't let his guys cause too much trouble with you around."

Levi smiled wryly. "I doubt he would, anyway. He seemed like he was really enjoying your company. And Sasha's."

Richard felt his gut tighten. "Well, he wasn't today, so I guess we'll see."

Levi didn't say anything else, he just gave Richard a long look before getting up and leaving the office.

When he was gone, Richard propped his forehead in his hands and sighed. He wanted to call Joey and figure out how to smooth things over between them, but he wasn't sure what the problem was in the first place, so how was he supposed to do that? Besides, it didn't really matter, did it? A few more days and Joey would be gone, back to Alabama or wherever, and Richard could get back to his normal life. Now that he thought about it, it felt like he'd been tied in knots for the last month, even though he'd only met Joey, what, a week ago? That was ridiculous.

He blamed Marshall Niven. Marshall's flirting had planted a seed in the back of Richard's mind, and then he'd met Joey, who was exactly the kind of guy to send Richard's libido into overdrive. It was pure coincidence, and that was the end of it.

"Just ride it out," Richard muttered to himself, opening a browser tab to check on a few banking items for Levi. "Just ride it out. He'll be gone in a couple of weeks, tops."

His voice sounded small and defiant in the quiet of the office.

By three the next morning, Richard had put the tension between himself and Joey out of his mind. Whatever it was, they could deal with it later. They were grown men, and there was nothing to keep them from being civil.

He hadn't been able to wipe the memory of that kiss away, though. No matter how involved he got with Sasha and her homework, no matter how hard he worked on sinking the first posts that would become a corral, the thought of it was there, floating in the back of his mind and threatening to derail his thoughts altogether. It wasn't uncomfortable, exactly...it was nerve-wracking. He felt out of control when he thought about it, like his body was going to go off and get involved with Joey without his permission. He shook his head and chuckled when he thought about it.

Now, early in the cold darkness of the unborn day, he noticed that Joey's big diesel wasn't in the driveway with the rest of the men. Richard figured he was just late, so he shrugged it off and hopped down out of the truck.

"Go on back home," Price said when he walked up to the rest of the men.

"What?" Richard asked, coming to a stop.

"Go on back home. Joey didn't call you?"

"Nope." Richard felt himself relax a little.

"Oh. Huh." It was Price's turn to shrug. "He had some kind of family thing, so he isn't going to make it. You can take the day off."

Richard looked toward the woods, the quadrant where he and Joey had been hunting. "I'll go ahead. I've hunted solo before."

Steve spoke up. "Naw, man. I don't think that's a good idea. Joey's rules."

Richard looked at him. There was no sense in going back home now. He was ready to go, and he'd already cleared his calendar of everything else for the week, so there wasn't much to do on the ranch. "Well, Joey isn't here, so I guess we're on our own."

Price held up both hands, as if to say he didn't want to argue.

"I'll just be careful," Richard said. "It's not like the coyotes will attack a grown man."

"They're getting pretty hungry," Price said, but Steve shook his head.

"You do what you want. I mean, this is more your ranch than ours. Just stay within your quadrant, all right? I don't want one of my guys accidentally shooting you."

"Got it," Richard said, turning away. "See you back here in a few hours."

The woods felt odd - too quiet and cold, a lot different than just the day before, when Joey had been beside him. It wasn't unnerving - he hadn't lied when he told those guys he was used to the woods, or that he had hunted alone. In fact, this morning was no different than a hundred other mornings when he'd been out here. The only difference was that he'd been hunting deer instead of coyotes. In other words, not that much difference. It had been a long time, though. He wasn't used to the emptiness of the dark woods or the quiet of the early morning. He'd get used to it.

He made his way up the mountainside, taking his time. It wasn't just the coyotes - there were a hundred ways to get hurt in the woods, some of them deadly. He wasn't about to risk his life, but he also didn't want to just go home, or sit at Levi's and drink coffee. He thought about all he'd learned from Joey and tried to decide whether to go to their original spot or find a new location to surprise the meandering pack. He wasn't sure.

It doesn't matter, some part of his mind nudged.

The thought surprised him so much that he stopped in his tracks on the trail and tried to figure out what it meant. Of course it mattered - the whole reason he was here was to hunt and kill coyotes. He should be able to do that better without the tension between him and Joey to distract him.

Right?

He thought about that first day, when he had volunteered to help. Had it really been just about Blueberry and Sasha? Of course that was part of it, but he knew damned well he could have found other ways to work off a payment for Levi. That was probably why Levi had looked at him so funny when he suggested it - coyote hunting was way out of Richard's wheelhouse.

And Joey was right, it was dangerous. So what really made Richard do it?

A picture of Joey, grinning at him like they were old buddies, flashed through his mind. Those steady, bright eyes, that made him look like he was hiding secrets. That strong face, framed with the ragged blond hair of a guy who looked like he didn't give a damn what you thought of him... And that swagger. Always that swagger, that said he was on top of the world and planned to stay there.

There was a lot there to like, and he knew it.

Hell, from the way Levi and Cruz stared at him every time Joey was in the vicinity, he guessed that everyone knew that and they expected him to...what? Notice? Because he did. Act on it? Maybe.

But how did a man do that? There was Sasha to consider, above all else. He had long ago made the decision to focus on her and keep her happy and safe, even at the cost of his own loneliness. Wasn't that what a good parent did? It was, and he refused to feel guilty about that.

Besides, Joey had some say in what happened between them, too, and now, after that kiss, he was gone. That said something about his attitude, and it wasn't a good sign. He knew there was some kind of emergency, but the situation spoke to Richard's deepest fear when it came to relationships - what happened when he and Sasha got firmly attached to someone and they just took off? What happened when they got tired of playing happy family and left him and his little girl in the dust, grieving over someone they loved.

Just like Alicia had done.

Richard winced, remembering the nights of Sasha crying for her mommy, the wondering where his wife had gone, the worry that something had happened to her. He remembered Alicia's voice, when it finally came days later. A voicemail. "I'm sorry, I can't. Go ahead without me. I won't bother you again."

That had been all, and that had been the night he made a decision to never share Sasha with anyone again. It was just too painful. Her little heart didn't need to be broken like that again, and it was his job to ensure it wouldn't.

Especially when it came to protecting her from someone like Joey, who made no secret of the fact that he came and went as he pleased. Whatever game Joey was playing, it didn't bode well for Richard and Sasha. Joey was a minefield that Richard refused to walk.

Chapter 16

Joey paced the cold corridor and checked the time on his phone again. He'd been checking it every two minutes since he left the motel, for no reason other than it made him feel better to do it. It sure wouldn't help save his brother.

"Joey? Joey Putnam?" a female voice said.

He turned to find a woman standing near the nurse's desk. She was wearing jeans, dirty cowboy boots and a ball cap. Her face was smudged with red dust. She definitely wasn't a nurse. "Yes? Who are you?"

Her face tried for a smile and didn't quite make it. "I'm Carrie."

He shook his head, but put two and two together right as she prompted, "Mack's wife?"

She stumbled over the word, like it was new to her. It was definitely new to Joey - the idea of Mack having a wife was beyond his imagination. "Oh, sure," he said. "Nice to meet you, I guess."

"He's still in surgery," she told him, gesturing toward a row of cold plastic seats near the windows. She glanced at them, pushing her hair out of her face with a small, trembling hand.

Outside, the night felt too dark and too cold, although it was nearly seventy on this Alabama night. A lot warmer than it would be in Comfort right now, for sure. Joey went and sat. Carrie followed him.

"What happened, exactly?" Joey asked, clasping his hands between his knees and leaning his elbows on his thighs. He watched her face, looking for any sign of...

134

What? What was he looking for, exactly? He didn't know anything about this girl, or her relationship with Mack. He needed to talk to Mack. "What happened? The nurse would only tell me that there was an accident."

Carrie sighed and slumped into the seat. Her eyes filled with tears and she blinked them away. She rubbed her hands on her thighs. "The tractor has needed work for a while now - I'm sure he told you. Something about the brakes. Anyway, he promised me that he wouldn't use it until I was home, but then he did it anyway and it...broke somehow. I'm not sure, exactly."

The tractor - the one Joey had been after Mack to replace for the last two years. It was one that had belonged to Cusp, an old Farmall that was about rusted through, last time he saw it. Mack had laughed it off and patted the big fender, calling the machine 'his old warhorse' and swearing it was fine.

Joey should have pushed harder. They had the money - he knew that for a fact. It was sitting there in the bank, waiting to be used on the farm. But for whatever reason, Mack hadn't liked spending it, and Joey never pushed it.

Now he wished he had. He opened his mouth to say something about that, then closed it again. He didn't know if Carrie here knew about that account, or if Mack had kept that to himself.

Then he shook his head, wondering what on earth he was thinking. Mack was the sweetest, most trusting and trustworthy guy on the planet. Of course he would tell his wife about everything. "So how bad is it?"

She shook her head. "I don't know yet. The doctor said the rear fender might have crushed a few bones, and there may be more internal injuries. I do know one lung was..." she hic-cupped... "punctured. He's in surgery now."

She squeezed her eyes closed. "I'm so glad it happened in the afternoon. Can you imagine him lying there all day, waiting for me to get home from school?"

Joey blinked. "School?"

"I'm a teacher. Didn't Mack tell you that?"

Joey shook his head. "We didn't talk about it much - I was in the middle of a job, and the news that he was married was just sort of... Well, it was kind of a shock. You know?"

Her smile was weak, but she nodded. Then she glanced to-ward the white double doors tucked back into a corner of the lobby. Joey glanced, too, but didn't see anything. "He's back there now?" he asked, nodding that direction.

"Yeah." Her voice trailed off and she blinked hard and swiped at her eyes with one hand. "He has huge plans, you know? I mean, really huge. He was so excited to tell you."

Joey frowned. "What kind of plans? I mean, he usually tells me everything." He smiled. "Boy never could keep a secret."

Then he realized what he was saying. "Well, except for now, I guess. He didn't tell me he was getting married."

She made a sound that was partly cry, partly laugh and hid her head in her hands for a moment. Behind her, a nurse called for someone on the intercom.

While Carrie got her emotions under control, he pulled out his phone, opened an app, and checked the balance in the farm account. It was all there - Mack hadn't even pulled the amount he normally used for general expenses. "Have you two been living on your salary?" he asked Carrie.

She shook her head. "No - his business is really starting to grow. He makes nearly as much as I do now."

Joey opened his mouth. Closed it again. Finally, confused, he asked, "What business?"

She put a hand to her mouth, eyes wide. "Oh. I'm sorry. That was another surprise. He wanted to tell you himself."

Joey sighed and pinched the bridge of his nose, then sat back and looked at the ceiling. "All right. Listen, Carrie. I don't know what's going to happen with Mack. Neither of us do. Since we don't know, is there any way you could catch me up to speed, as far as him and the farm? I mean, I know you want to respect his wishes, but I'm really feeling out of the loop here."

"Well, maybe you should have come home more often," she said, her voice stronger. "He misses you like crazy, Joey. You're his best friend. He wanted to show you his work, and he wanted to tell you how well he's doing."

That stung. "I know. And I'll apologize for that as soon as I can." At least she was concerned about Mack's welfare, and his feelings. That was heartening to hear, even if it made Joey ashamed of himself for not being there as much as he should have been. "But for now, could you fill me in?"

For the first time since he had gotten the call from the sheriff, Joey felt desperate. Mack was his only brother, the only family he had left in the world, now that Cusp was gone, and he had walked away from it all, more or less. He'd just expected the farm to be there, expected Mack to be there. He had assumed that everything would go on as it always had, for as long as he wanted it to. That was selfish and stupid, but he wasn't sure if it was too late to fix it.

She clutched at her stomach with both arms, rocking back and forth, then sat up with a tiny laugh. "All right, but if Mack gets mad, I'm telling him you made me."

"Fair enough. I'll take the heat for that."

"I met Mack at the vocational school. He was there taking welding classes, and we started having lunch together every day."

"Why were you there?" Joey asked.

Her eyebrows came up. "Teacher, remember? Try to focus." She softened the words with a smile. "Anyway, we really hit it off. I mean, I've never met anyone like Mack before, and he just..." She shook her head. "Captivated me. I know how that sounds, but it's true. I caught myself thinking about him a lot. All the time."

"So you started dating?"

"Well, not at first, because I was busy. I hold classes for re-medial adult students, but because a lot of them work, I keep an evening schedule, too. So I didn't have much time."

She was looking past him, toward the window. He could see her reflection, across from his own. Outside on the side-walk, a few people were coming and going, but no one looked in at them.

"But eventually, yeah. We started dating." She paused. "He was worried about you, you know," she said.

He frowned. "What? Why?"

She shrugged. "He said you were lost - that was the way he put it. He said you hadn't found your wonderful yet."

"I...don't know what that means."

"Me, either, but that's what he always said. Anyway, we started getting serious, and he finally let me come to the farm - your farm, I guess."

"Our farm. You mean he hadn't let you see it?"

She shook her head. "Not that he didn't want to, but he wanted you to be there, I think." She looked at her hands. "He wanted to show me everything important in his life, all at once."

Wow. Joey nearly cringed at that one. It sounded exactly like Mack, and now he felt even worse. She might as well have been talking about a complete stranger. Joey hadn't known Mack was taking classes. He hadn't known about Carrie. He hadn't known about any business. Mack had always been...not a follower, exactly, but content to go along and not rock the boat. Cusp had always prodded him to speak up, to take his place in the world, but Mack would simply grin at him and then do his own thing.

Joey had taken advantage of that nature more than once, as the older brother. Hell, Cusp had encouraged it to a small degree, hoping that Mack would see what was happening and fight back. He wanted Mack to stand up for himself, wanted to know that when he was gone, 'his boys' as he so proudly called them, were capable of facing a world that was hard and cold, in his estimation.

Now, listening to Carrie talk, Joey realized that all Mack needed was a good reason to find his gumption, and that Carrie herself was that reason. Interesting.

"There was a lot of blood," Carrie said, her voice breaking. She looked like she might be ready to cry again, but she held back. "He was going in and out of consciousness, like it was too hard to stay with me until the rescue squad got there. I was so scared..." She looked away from Joey, toward the doors.

Joey looked too, then said, "The longer it takes, the better it is - it means they're still working. He's still alive."

She slumped against the arm of the chair and tried to smile at him. They were quiet for a moment. She seemed lost in her worry, and Joey didn't know what to say next. The two of them took turns glancing toward the doors that hid Mack from view.

"He was doing well," she said, "But he worried about you."

Joey stared at her. "Me? Why?"

She ducked her head, shy. "He said you weren't happy. That you were so successful, but you didn't have anyone to share it with, and that made you sad, deep down."

"He's wrong. I'm perfectly happy with my life. It was Mack we always worried about."

He shifted in his seat and looked out the window, watching people hurry by. Storm clouds were moving in from the west, and the trees were starting to whip around.

He wanted to go outside, get some fresh air. No, it wasn't a want - he needed to go. Needed to take a deep breath and stretch his legs. "I'll be back in a minute," he said, standing up.

She nodded and stood up, too. He was afraid she would follow him, but she asked, "You want some coffee? I'm going to the cafeteria."

He nodded and watched her walk down the hall, then followed the arrows on the floor to a door that led out into a courtyard. The small square of green space with benches in the corners was deserted, which was good. He didn't like the turn Carrie's conversation had taken, and he needed a minute to himself.

Who was she to decide Mack was right about him? For that matter, how would Mack know if Joey was happy or not? Other than the occasional visit and more or less weekly phone calls, they never really talked. When they did, it was about the farm or money or random stuff that had no real impact on their lives. Joey couldn't remember the last time they had any sort of deep, meaningful conversation. Probably when Cusp died. They had both been devastated over that, and it had taken a while to get their heads on straight.

Of course, Carrie wouldn't know any of this. She was just repeating what Mack told her. That thought didn't make him less uncomfortable.

But was she right? Was Mack right? Joey leaned against a concrete wall and kicked at a clump of grass, thinking it over. If one of his guys had tried to tell him he wasn't happy, he would have laughed it off. But for some reason, the idea that Mack thought so gave the idea more weight. They might not talk much but, to his surprise, Joey found that he was considering it.

Of course Mack was, as usual, seeing everything through rose-colored glasses. Probably even more so now that he was married. He would want others to be as happy as him. Alex, Joey's employee, wouldn't shut up about how happy he was when he got engaged. Same thing, right? The whole crew was relieved when he finally went on his honeymoon, hoping he'd get it out of his system.

It was definitely the same thing. Mack just wanted everyone else to be as happy as him and Carrie. But Joey was perfectly fine with life as it was working out. He didn't need a life partner just because everyone else seemed to be finding theirs. Hell, he wasn't even looking.

Chapter 17

Richard spent the morning thinking, without a single coyote in sight. By the time the sun rose, he was cursing his boredom and wishing he'd gone back home when Price suggested it. By mid-morning, he was done. Gathering his Thermos and rifle, he gave up on the idea of making a kill and headed down the mountain. But when he got to the trail intersection that led upward, to the orchard, he took it on a whim, wanting to see the valley from the top of the mountain. There was no hurry to get home.

The trees were starting to green, more than just a week ago when he was up here with Joey. He sat on a large flat rock and watched the birds, enjoying the solitude. He wondered why he didn't bring Sasha up here more often, but then remembered that anytime she got near the ranch, she only wanted to ride. He smiled at that and shook his head.

But thinking about Sasha and riding, he realized he needed to get back down the mountain. There was fencing to be reinforced and a corral to be built, now that Blueberry was hers. Time to get going.

He was just stepping down over the lip of the mountain when he lost his footing and fell. A tree root, thick and round and jutting at just the right angle to tip his balance when he stepped on it, sent him sprawling downward, into the trees below the orchard. He yelped when it happened and again when his shoulder butted the trunk of an old birch. Something in the side of his neck popped and pain shot through his shoulder.

It stopped his fall, mostly, but when he rolled to a stop, groaning, he was in enough pain that he rolled over and nearly threw up. When he tried to sit up, dizziness swamped him and he laid back against the tree. The idea of standing made him even sicker. He thought it might be best to just sit still and let it pass, especially with the tunnel vision that kept threatening to knock him out completely.

He reached for the radio, then changed his mind. The crew was busy with their duties. They didn't have time to come rescue his butt right now. It would screw up their hunt for the whole day, once they started moving around the woods.

When he'd started out this morning, the air felt crisp and clean. Now, sitting on the ground, a real chill was creeping up into his bones and making his teeth chatter. He needed to get home.

He tried pushing up off the ground, but it was nearly impossible with just one working arm. Next he tried pulling up with the trunk of the tree, and that worked better. Once he was on his feet, the gut-twisting nausea came back, so he leaned there for a few moments.

Motion in his peripheral vision caught his eye. When he looked, he caught the smallest glimpse of a curled gray tail as it disappeared into the brush. He pushed up onto unsteady feet, winced at the pain in his arm, and raised his rifle halfway. If he was mistaken, he didn't want to accidentally aim at one of the crew or some other human. If he wasn't, he wanted to be ready.

Right now, injured, he was considered prey, and he didn't like that feeling at all.

There was no more movement in the area, beyond the trees blowing, and after a few minutes he relaxed his stance.

All right, now to get home. He only had himself, his rifle, and...he looked down at the Thermos that had rolled ten feet away and landed in an indentation in the earth. Maybe he'd come back for it, because he sure as hell wasn't carrying it off the mountain today. He could barely carry himself off the mountain, and he still wasn't sure he was going to be successful.

He really, really wished he'd heeded Price's warning this morning. He wished he'd taken Joey more seriously, too. Sure, he'd gone hunting plenty of times alone, but it only took one bad day to get a man into real trouble. He knew that in theory before, but now he knew it in fact.

He pulled out his phone and checked the time. Ten-fifteen. Another two hours at least before the other men got back to the ranch and realized he wasn't there.

If they realized. They might easily assume he'd headed on home early.

Better to get started than wait around for help. Those storm clouds were starting to pile up.

Nausea threatened his stomach again, but he tried to ignore it. What he needed was a walking stick of some kind, to keep him on his feet whenever the dizziness hit him. He tried two that were relatively close, but they both broke under his weight. Maybe he could find something farther down the trail.

At least he was going downhill. That should make things a lot easier.

He thought he caught movement again, and this time he was sure he saw gray fur among the darker bark of the trees. This was close to the spot he and Joey had taken down the female coyote, so it would make sense - he was blocking the trail to their den. They probably avoided him for a while, until they realized that he was injured. Now they were curious, moving in to see what was going on.

Richard was suddenly very aware of the danger he was courting in this situation. Not that the coyotes - what did Joey call them? Songdogs? Not that the songdogs were a threat as long as he was awake and watching, because a couple of well-placed rifle shots would most likely scare them off. He was more worried about what might happen if the dizziness and tunnel vision from the pain overtook him. In other words, if he passed out. Which felt like a very real possibility.

No shooting then. No nothing. If they were as hungry as he thought, they would be on him too fast and there wouldn't be one thing he could do about it.

Even if it wasn't the dogs, the cold drizzling rain might get him. Maybe not right now, but this kind of weather settled into the bones and burned the lungs. It suppressed the immune system, he knew, opening the door to any number of illnesses. He was shivering as it was, and he knew he couldn't stay out here too much longer.

The hunt be damned. He pulled the radio from his pocket and keyed up. "Price, you copy?" he asked into the mike.

No answer. He tried again.

Nothing.

Well, hell. He looked at the radio and frowned. It was working. He even pressed the button a few times to make sure.

But his hands were starting to ache from the cold, and his shivering was getting worse. He put it into his pocket and pulled out his cell phone. Made a call. "Levi, I'm just down the trail from the orchards. I think I need some help up here."

"What's up, bud? You got..."

That was all Richard heard before the phone slipped from his hand, but it was enough. He sat hard on the ground, fell back against a tree and closed his eyes, holding his rifle across his lap with both hands.

It wasn't until hours later he came to. He was in a vehicle, under a blanket, lying on something hard but pretty comfy, so he went back to sleep. Not that he had that much of a choice. His eyes closed without his permission.

Chapter 18

"He thinks you got the wrong idea about family from old Cusp," Carrie was saying to Joey as he paced the waiting room. "He wants you to find love and be happy."

"I am happy," Joey said, trying to keep from snapping at her. None of this had anything to do with her, and she didn't deserve his attitude. But Mack was wrong. Joey liked his life. Just because Mack felt better as a settled man, that didn't mean Joey would.

For some reason the thought of Richard came to mind. Him and Sasha at Richard's ranch the other night. It all seemed so peaceful. So happy. Maybe if Joey met a guy like Richard, he would think about rearranging his life like that.

You just did, he reminded himself. Richard actually is that guy.

He considered this. He felt like he had a real connection to Richard, but that wasn't enough to mean anything. It was true that Joey had liked being there, had loved Richard and Sasha's company, had felt perfectly at home at their house. He could easily see himself fitting in there, becoming part of the family.

He shook his head. Richard was already settled. He had a child and a life and a home in North Carolina. Besides, when Joey had kissed him the other night - an impulsive but delicious decision - Richard had nearly gone into shock. Joey got the distinct impression that he wasn't interested.

On the other hand, there were moments during this past week when Joey was positive he saw real interest in Richard's eyes.

He opened his mouth to tell Carrie that Mack was wrong when someone in scrubs came through the double doors and called, "Mrs. Putnam?"

Joey and Carrie both whirled toward the woman, who looked completely flushed and exhausted, but calm. A doctor, Joey thought. She looked like a doctor. Joey wondered if that was a good or bad sign, but all he did was glance toward Carrie and follow her.

"I'm Doctor Newman," the woman said. "I do need to sit down, if you don't mind."

"Of course," Carrie said. Once they were all seated in the waiting room chairs, she said, "Mack? Is he all right?"

Dr. Newman nodded. Then she said, "We've done our very best with him. We've placed steel rods in both legs and one of his upper arms. We had to do our best to patch up his ribs. Those are going to hurt for a while, but at least he didn't puncture a lung, like we thought." She paused and looked at Joey, then Carrie. "He's going to need a lot of help for a while. This won't be a quick or easy healing process. But he will, eventually, be fine."

Carrie let out her breath and slumped into her chair.

"He's in recovery now, and we aren't quite out of the woods yet, but the worst is over." The doctor stood and turned away. "If you'll excuse me."

"Wait. Can we see him?" Joey asked.

The doctor shook her head. "Not yet. Go get something to eat and come back in a couple of hours. He should be awake then."

Then she was gone, leaving Carrie and Joey looking at each other, neither of them knowing what to say. Finally, Carrie sighed. "Whatever it takes, I'll do it. If Mack needs round the clock care, I'll quit my job. If he needs special accommodations, we'll figure it out." She shrugged, but there was steely determination in her eyes when she looked at Joey.

Joey's eyebrows came up. "You sure about that?" he asked.

"Of course I'm sure," she said, picking her purse up from the chair. As she walked by, she leaned closer and looked him dead in the eye. "When you love someone, that's what you do. You heard the lady - let's get some food."

He watched her walk out of the room, then followed. With news that Mack would be OK, she looked brighter than she had even a few minutes ago. Even with the obvious problems that would follow. Even with him not being as healthy as he was. Joey knew then that he'd been wrong - Carrie definitely loved his brother. He felt his own shoulders relax at the realization.

They grabbed trays and a few of the meager offerings in the cafeteria, then found a table near the wall of windows. There weren't too many people here, and most of them looked like staff. A low murmur of conversation filled the room and no one looked up at them when they sat down. Outside, the day had grown brighter.

Carrie was looking at the contents of her sandwich, chuckling about something, when Joey's phone rang. It was Levi, and before he could say more than hello, Levi was yelling.

"What do you mean, leaving one of my men in the woods hurt?" he was saying, catching Joey totally off guard. "I ought to have you arrested."

"What?" Joey asked. "Wait - Levi, wait." He glanced at Carrie and then got up and went outside. "Levi. What happened?"

"What do you mean, what happened? Richard's your partner, and he's in the hospital. You tell me what happened, or so help me..."

"Wait." Joey had to practically yell to get him to listen. "Levi, I'm in Alabama. I don't know what happened to Richard."

He had an idea, even before Levi told him. He forgot to call and cancel. He bet that Richard, determined to pay off that damned horse, had gone anyway, directly against Joey's rules.

"We found him unconscious in the woods. He's frozen stiff."

"Was he hunting?"

"Well, he sure as hell wasn't playing hopscotch," Levi snapped. "I want you and your men gone from my ranch by the end of the day. You hear me?"

"Levi, I had no idea -."

"I don't care." Levi's voice was cold. He hung up.

Joey looked at the phone. OK, they could work this out somehow. Maybe once Levi calmed down...

Richard was hurt, though? How had that happened? His heart thudded in his chest. Was he all right? He pulled up his phone menu to call Steve and find out more, but before he could, the number from the Broken Blue flashed onto his Caller ID.

He didn't want to answer it, if he was going to get yelled at some more. With a small sigh, he did anyway. "Hello?"

It was Cruz. "Joey, Levi is upset, but please don't take his words to heart. He'll calm down after a while."

"It doesn't matter if he calms down. He's ordered me off his land," Joey said, hoping against hope that Cruz could talk Levi down from his tree. Joey didn't want to lose this job.

"Just...lay low for a while. Can you do that?"

"Cruz, what happened to Richard? Is he all right?"

"I think he will be. It's hypothermia and a dislocated shoulder, as best I can tell. Lots of cuts and bruises, but nothing too serious there. He shouldn't have been out there alone, and until he decides to tell us, we won't know why he decided to do something so stupid."

"All right. Thanks for letting me know. I'll pull my crew from the job for now."

"Probably a good idea, but don't go too far. Like I said, Levi will calm down once Richard talks to him."

"What about Sasha?" Joey asked.

"Oh." A smile lit Cruz's voice. "She's here with us. We're making cookies for your shindig this weekend."

Joey frowned. He'd forgotten all about that, and now that he remembered, he doubted it would happen.

Joey hung up and realized that Carrie was staring at him. "Is everything all right?" she asked. "For a moment there you looked like your best friend had died."

He opened his mouth, then closed it again. "Not my best friend," he murmured finally.

"Someone important, though," she said, pointing her plastic fork at him. "I can see it on your face."

"Yeah," he said quietly. The thought of Sasha, worried about her Daddy, and Richard, alone and hurt in the woods, tugged at him. "Someone important."

He briefly explained what was going on.

"I'm sorry."

"Let's go see Mack for a minute," he answered, "Then I'll take off and deal with this other thing."

Chapter 19

Mack's eyes were glowing when Joey and Carrie came through the door, even though his normally crazed curls were plastered to the sides of his face and he was as pale as the pillow under his head.

"Man," he said, struggling to sit up as Joey leaned down to give him a hug, "These drugs are outstanding."

Joey laughed. Even under these circumstances, it was good to see his little brother. He stood back so that Carrie could hug him, too. She did, and then sat on the edge of his bed. Joey noticed that she wouldn't let go of his hand, either. She looked like she might weep.

"You scared us to death, boy," Joey said. "What were you thinking, using that deathtrap instead of buying a new machine?"

Mack made a face. "I like the old warhorse. It has character."

"What it has, is too many problems. Pick out something new, and I'll have it delivered."

Mack shook his head. When he spoke, Joey could hear the slight softness in his voice, like he was not quite awake yet. "Nope. You need to save your money."

"I've got money."

"You're going to need more."

"Why?"

Mack glanced up at Carrie and smiled. "Because one day you're going to find someone who makes you as happy as Carrie makes me, and you're going to want to start a life together. You'll need money to do that."

"Mack..." Joey started, but stopped when the image of Richard and Sasha flashed through his mind again.

Mack was staring at him. So was Carrie. "You already did, didn't ya? You dog."

Joey shook his head. "No, I -."

"Don't lie to me." Mack smiled wider. "I know you. I can tell."

"You're on drugs. You just said so." Joey crossed his arms and leaned against the doorway.

Mack waved a hand. "Whatever. I'm glad you came, even if I had to bang myself up to get you here."

Joey refused to feel guilty. "Why are you riding me? What did I do?"

"Nothing." Mack was still smiling, but his smile was softer again, and he was looking at Carrie, not him. "I'm just giving you grief."

It felt different, being with Mack, Joey thought. Something had changed, but he wasn't sure what.

"You still up for letting us buy you out?" Mack asked.

"We don't need to talk about that right now..."

Mack's eyebrows came up. "Yes we do, because the minute I get better, you'll be gone again, and we won't see you for another six months."

Carrie stopped looking at Mack long enough to offer Joey a shrug.

"Actually, I've got to get out of here this afternoon. I've got a temporary hire in North Carolina, and he got hurt today, too."

"Uh-oh."

"I don't think it's a big deal, but I need to get back there and make sure." But it was a big deal, because of Sasha.

"Isn't Steve there to handle it?" Mack asked.

"Yeah. I just want to take care of it myself."

"What's his name? The guy who got hurt?"

"Richard. He's got a daughter named Sasha. Cute kid, and he can't afford to be out of commission because of her."

Mack didn't answer. Instead he looked up at Carrie. "That's the one," he said. She nodded her agreement.

Joey looked back and forth between them. "The one what? What are you two talking about?"

"Your voice went all gushy when you said his name. You relaxed, too. This Richard guy is important to you."

"No - I just don't want him hurt. What's wrong with that?"

"Nothing, but it's more than that. If nothing else, he's got your interest."

Joey sighed. "Look, Mack. I love ya, man, but you don't know what you're talking about. There is no 'the one', first of all. There's just me. Second, you don't know my life right now, so you don't know if I'm going to settle down anytime soon or not."

"Answer one question," Mack said.

"What?" Joey sighed.

He really, really wanted to get out of here. Jump in the truck and head back to the Broken Blue. Apparently Carrie had given Mack some...something. Backbone? Courage? Joey wasn't sure which, but Mack sure was a lot more assertive than the last time Joey was here, and he didn't like it all that much.

"Have you slept with anyone since you met him?" Mack asked.

Joey shook his head. "What has that got to do with -?"

"Have you?" The teasing grin on Mack's face told Joey he already knew the answer.

"No. I haven't. Because I've been busy."

Mack laughed out loud at that, the laugh ending in a hiss and plenty of, "Ow, owowow, ow." He clutched his belly and tried to bend forward, which resulted in more moaning. Carrie reached to help him, but he waved his hand and smiled at her. "Sorry, babe, I'm good." She still fluffed at his pillow for a moment before she went back to her spot on the edge of the bed.

Joey watched them, thinking that maybe his worries about Mack were unfounded. In fact, if anything, Mack seemed less gullible than before. Maybe there was real good between the two of them.

"Honey, would you do me a favor and go ask the nurse when I can have pain meds?" Mack asked Carrie, but he was looking at Joey.

She looked at Joey too, smiled, and left with a "Sure thing," thrown over one shoulder.

"What do you think?" Mack asked when she was gone. "Isn't she amazing?"

"Umm, I guess? I don't know, Mack. If you think so, that's all that matters."

"Cusp would have liked her, I think," Mack said.

Joey nodded. "Yeah, probably. She's good to you, right? I mean, you didn't just get her out of the room to tell me she was holding you hostage or anything?"

Mack started to laugh again, but managed to keep it easy so it didn't hurt. "No. She's the best thing that ever happened to me. And I'm serious about wanting to buy out the farm."

Joey nodded. "I know. You sound serious."

"I'm just...happy. Maybe you don't get it, but it's true. I want to do everything right for us, you know?"

"Well, take the farm."

"What?" Mack frowned and blinked.

"I said, take the farm. It's yours. On one condition."

"What condition?"

"You'll let me have that new tractor delivered this week. I won't give you the place if it's going to kill you."

"Fine," Mack laughed. "But you can't just give me the farm."

"Yes I can."

It was true. Joey was never there anyway, and if it made Mack this happy, then...

"I mean, I won't let you do that. I told you, I want to do this right. I've been saving up, and I want to earn it."

"You have earned it - that place would be a useless mess without you there to take care of it."

"Nope. I'm buying it. I won't accept it otherwise."

"Consider it my wedding present?" Joey asked hopefully.

"Nope."

"Fine." Joey pinched the bridge of his nose and hung his head. "How much do you have saved up?"

"Nearly ten grand, but I'm still working on it."

"Give me five, then pay me a hundred bucks a month. Sound good?"

"Uh...yes? But I can do better than that."

"Who cares?"

"I do. Joey, you don't get to dictate terms and then I'll just follow along. It doesn't work that way anymore."

Mack gingerly moved to grab a pen and paper that was laying on the table beside his bed. Joey reached to help him, and once he was settled again, Mack started scribbling, while Joey watched.

Finally Mack handed him the paper to read. "Is that all right with you?" he asked.

Joey looked at the numbers, and then looked at Mack. He nodded. "Yep, if you think you can do that."

"I can. It'll be work, but I want to own the place outright before planting next spring."

"All right. You got it. Take it to Barnes," he said, meaning their lawyer. "I'll sign it."

"Good. Thanks, Joey."

Joey shot him a salute and turned to go. "No problem, little brother. As long as it makes you happy."

"It does. And Joey?"

"Yeah?"

"Start thinking about what makes you happy, all right?"

"Will do." Joey finally escaped the room, saying a quick goodbye to Carrie, who was waiting at the nurse's station, and then made his way down to his truck. Once inside, he slammed the door and put his head on the steering wheel.

The trip back to North Carolina was a killer. In between thinking about Mack and his new wife, and worrying about Richard, he had to contend with his own thoughts about what Mack had said. The radio didn't help - lots of love songs. So many love songs. Everybody was in love, it seemed, but him. His guys all had wives and girlfriends, Levi had Cruz, Mack had Carrie, and hell, even Richard had Sasha - not that that was exactly the same. But he loved her, Joey could tell. They had each other.

Loneliness wasn't an emotion Joey was very familiar with, and he decided that he didn't like it at all.

No, wait. That wasn't true. Now that he thought about it, loneliness, this emotion that he was feeling right now, was the same one he felt whenever he picked up some company in whatever town he was working. It was the emotion he felt when he called home and heard Mack jabbering about the farm.

He was crossing the North Carolina state line when he realized it was the emotion he felt the other night, watching Richard and Sasha together, working with the horse, walking their land, and talking about their day.

His mind latched onto Cory, and he decided that tonight, once he got back to the motel, he would take him up on his offer of company. That was all that was wrong, he thought. He hadn't had any company since he got here, and he just needed something to scratch the itch. That would solve the problem. Simple.

So why didn't it feel simple? Why did it feel so...

Cheap.

Like it was too easy, too slippery. Like there was nothing under the surface.

But that was the way he liked it, he reminded himself, reaching to flip off the radio. No strings attached, no irritation. Nothing to hold him back.

That was the best way to live. Hell, married guys in the suburbs dreamed of living his life - a free bird, with the best job in the world, money in the bank, and no one to question his comings and goings.

No one at all.

"Damn it," he said, in the silence of the truck.

Maybe he needed to get a dog. Then again, that would be stupid, because he was on the road so much that he'd have to board it all the time. So no dog.

Besides, he was homeless.

The thought startled him. He was, actually. He'd just sold the only place he ever called home to Mack.

"That means I'm free to go wherever I want. I can buy a place in Vegas. I can move to Texas. I could even -." He realized he was talking to himself and shut up.

He passed by the gates to the Broken Blue and drove on into Comfort. The hospital sign came into view and his heart sped up a little. He hoped that Richard was all right. He hoped that...well, he didn't know what he hoped, exactly, but he knew that he wouldn't feel right until he saw the man and confirmed for himself that he was going to be fine.

The hospital, like the one in Alabama, was too bright and too quiet. His boots clunked along the corridor, making him wince with every step. He found Levi and Sasha before he found Richard's room. They were standing in the hall and turned when they heard him coming. Levi's face went dark, but Sasha smiled and said, "Mr. Putnam! You're here!"

"I'm here. I heard your dad got hurt," he said, taking her hand and squeezing it.

"Levi said he's going to be all right," she told him. Her hair was back in a ponytail and her eyes shone up at him. She looked tired. She also looked like she wasn't sure she believed what the grown-ups were telling her.

"I'm sure he is," Joey said, glancing at Levi. "How is he?"

"He'll be all right. Hypothermia and a dislocated shoulder, like I said before." Levi grimaced. "I spoke to him for a few minutes earlier. Sorry I snapped at you."

Joey shrugged. "You were worried. I would have done the same, most likely."

"Does dislocated mean lost?" Sasha asked.

"Nope, I think that's unlocated. Dislocated means it's still there, but not in the right spot," Joey answered. "Can I see him?"

"He's asleep," Levi said, but then shrugged. "At least he was a few minutes ago."

Joey looked down at Sasha. "Can I go see your daddy?"

"Yes. He already asked where you were. Didn't he, Uncle Levi?"

"Yeah." Levi turned away and said, "C'mon, kiddo. Let's go get something to drink."

Joey watched them go and then carefully pushed open the door to Richard's room. It looked a lot like Mack's room, to be honest, with the exception of the extra person in the bed by the window, an old man who looked over at him with a scowl when he came in.

Richard looked at him, too, and Joey's breath actually caught in his throat. His naturally darker skin was stark against the sheets, and his expression was flat and tired, so different from the animated and smiling guy that Joey had come to know. His attempt at a smile was slow and sleepy.

"Hey, man," Joey said, looking around for a chair and pulling an ugly blue one to the edge of the bed. "How are you?"

Richard tried to chuckle and made a flipping motion with his hand. "Meh."

"I take it you went hunting this morning." Joey smiled, relieved to see that Richard was alive and well. He knew he should be angry, but he wasn't.

"Yeah. About that..." Richard looked down.

Joey laughed softly.

"Listen," Richard said, pushing with one arm to sit up straighter in the bed. His other arm folded over his lap.

Joey jumped up to help him, putting an arm around his waist. Richard adjusted his weight while Joey lifted, and together they got him into a more comfortable position. When Joey moved to sit down again, Richard grabbed his arm. "Joey?"

Joey stopped and looked up, directly into Richard's eyes. He was so close that the memory of their kiss flashed through his mind. He was deeply aware of the heat of Richard's body and the faint smell of some woodsy shampoo from his hair. Mostly he was aware of the weight between them, the something unsaid, undone. The something that he wanted to do.

He licked his lips and cleared his throat. "Yeah?" he asked, his voice too high.

"I just wanted to say I'm sorry. I know it was stupid..."

Joey blinked, still thinking about Richard's eyes and lips, how he tasted. "What?"

"Going into the woods on my own like I did? You know. Disregarding your direction."

"Oh." Joey heaved a breath and pulled back. "That. Yeah, well...bet you won't do that again."

He tried to laugh and make a joke out of it, but he didn't quite get there. "I'm just glad you're OK. I mean it."

Richard looked down. "I know you do."

Joey froze with his butt halfway to the seat. There was something in Richard's voice. A small hitch, a softening of his words.

Joey looked at him, but he was still looking down. Had Richard wanted him to kiss him, just then? The idea of it sent a small shiver of desire down Joey's spine. "Richard?" he prodded. "What do you mean?"

Instead of answering, Richard held out his good hand and placed it on Joey's stubbled jaw. Just for a moment, then he pulled away again. "What happened between us the other night..." he said. Then he stopped.

"Yeah?" Joey stood again and planted himself on the edge of Richard's bed. His heart was stammering against his ribs and he couldn't draw a full breath. "Richard?"

It was his turn to hold out a hand. He touched Richard's chin with a knuckle and lifted it until their eyes met. What he saw in Richard's gaze nearly made him gasp.

"I wanted it," Richard said quietly. "Hell, I needed it."

"You sure?" Joey heard the hesitation in his words.

"Yes. You showed me how lonely I've been. And how sometimes -." Here he smiled a little. "Sometimes I need to hang out with adults."

"Like me?"

"Like you. I'm sure you're not the kind of guy who gets all soft and stuff, but I really do want to know you better."

"What..." Joey stopped. Tried to think past the singing in his chest. "What makes you think I don't like soft?"

"You live like a nomad, from what you've told me. I get that. Hell, I would, too, if not for Sasha. You like -."

"You don't know what I like," Joey said, leaning forward, careful of Richard's arm, and stealing a soft kiss. "I like you. I've liked you from the moment we met."

Richard's breath smelled like toothpaste. "I like you, too," he said.

"I like Sasha, too. And Levi and Cruz." Joey smiled "Hell, I even like Blueberry."

Richard laughed out loud then, and it sounded sweet to Joey's ears. "I want to make you laugh more," he said. "I like to hear you laugh."

"I need to laugh more." Richard paused, and a shadow crossed his face. "But how much longer will you even be around, Joey?"

Joey wanted to be honest here. He also wanted to say exactly the right thing to make this amazing possibility a reality. "I do have to work, but I can take some time if I want, after this job is finished for Levi. I was already planning on it, in fact."

"Oh, yeah?" The smile was back, tickling the corners of Richard's mouth. Joey wanted to kiss it.

"Yeah. I planned on going home...Well, to my brother's place, I guess. But as it turns out, he likes his new wife better than he likes me. I'm kind of homeless."

"You could spend some time with us," Richard offered, but there was worry in his voice, even though he tried to hide it.

"What? Would that be a problem?"

Richard looked away, toward the door.

"Richard? Talk to me."

"I'm just afraid," he said. "For Sasha. She tends to get attached to the men in her life. You see how she is with Levi and Cruz and the other hands."

"Oh." Joey frowned. "You mean I haven't even shown up yet and you're kicking me out?"

"Oh. No. I just...have to be careful, for her sake."

Joey scooted closer. Took Richard's good hand in his. "Listen to me. I may be a despicable, lowdown homeless bum, but I would never hurt a little girl. Especially her. She's a doll-baby. But you have to be willing to take that chance. You have to say yes or no. I don't know how the story plays out, but neither do you."

Richard nodded slowly. "You're right. I don't know the future. I have to either be alone until she's out of the house, or take a chance."

Joey chuckled. "That about sums it up." He kissed Richard again and squeezed his hand. "You think about it, all right? I've got to go check in with my men and get some sleep."

Richard nodded. Joey felt his eyes on him all the way out the door.

Levi and Sasha were standing outside, looking at the treats in the snack machine. "Everything all right?" Levi asked as he walked by.

"Just fine. I'll see you in the morning."

Joey got in his truck and headed toward the motel, letting Richard's words run through his mind over and over. After he met up with his crew and locked himself in his room, he texted his brother. *You got to me. I'm in trouble now.*

He fell asleep thinking that he didn't need Cory, or anyone else for that matter. He only wanted Richard, and he knew that would be enough.

Chapter 20

"**M**an, would you take it easy?" Richard snapped at Levi, holding onto the arms of the wheelchair for dear life. Sasha ran along beside him, giggling. Levi was flying down the hall, pushing Richard and doing wheelies whenever the notion struck. "I'm gonna get hurt worse here than I did in the woods."

Beside them, a nurse tried to keep up, shooting glares at Levi's shoulder, which Levi successfully ignored. "Sir?" she said. "Mr. King?"

Richard stared straight ahead.

"What? And don't call me that, Rhonda. We've known each other since the third grade."

"Hospital protocol," she mumbled. "Please be careful with him. You're going to cost me my job."

That, thankfully, slowed him down a little, and Richard relaxed. Sasha slowed down, too. "Can I ride in your lap, Daddy?" she asked.

"Not with Levi driving, you can't. I want you to make it to your eighth birthday."

"I'll be careful with her," Levi promised.

"But not me?" Richard tried to twist around and look at him, but it didn't work. He only managed to hurt his badly bruised shoulder. "If you kill me, Cruz'll be doing your taxes this year."

Levi groaned.

Sasha said, "You have taxis?"

It was a gorgeous Saturday morning, almost warm enough to say that spring was in the air. Getting Richard into the truck was nearly as hair-raising as the wheelchair ride. Finally, in a fit of impatience, Levi simply picked Richard up and dropped him onto the rear bench seat.

"Hey!" Richard said, grabbing onto the seat.

Sasha laughed hard, and he smiled at her. "You are having way too much fun with this, little girl."

"Uncle Levi picked you up like a baby!" she squealed.

Levi laughed, plopped Sasha into the front passenger seat, and closed the doors.

"He picked you up like a baby, too," Richard teased her, watching to make sure she belted herself in. He was glad to be going home, glad that Sasha seemed happy. He was afraid she'd be scared when she found out he'd gotten hurt, but Levi and Cruz had managed to keep her distracted. "Did you take care of Blueberry?" he asked. "Food, water? Did you ride him?"

"Yes, Daddy. Of course I did. Pam took me over this morning."

"Good. I'm proud of you."

Levi got behind the wheel and slammed the door. "That nurse was mean."

"Rhonda was concerned. Not mean. Do you blame her, there, Earnhardt?"

Levi shrugged, started the truck, and backed out. "I'll be glad to get you home. You're grouchy."

"Uncle Cruz said I had to take good care of you, Dad. He said to make you behave, too."

Levi chuckled. "I bet you'll have some help with that," he told Sasha.

"What do you mean?" Richard asked.

"Joey Putnam has called me four times today, to find out when you're coming home," Levi said. "I get the feeling he'll be there soon, if he isn't there already."

That made Richard smile, and he settled back into the seat. What happened between him and Joey was still on his mind, and had been since it happened two days ago. He still wasn't sure what to think about the whole thing, but he knew he damned well liked it. He hoped Joey would stick around, so they could explore this new facet of their relationship. After those kisses, Richard couldn't deny that he wanted more. A lot more.

"Are you all right?" Levi asked, glancing at him in the rearview mirror. "Your face is all red."

Richard bit back a grin. "I'm good."

He watched as Levi pulled into his driveway. He was glad to see that someone brought his truck home, and he was equally glad to see the big diesel with the man leaning against it, as if he'd been waiting there for a while.

"Mr. Putnam is here, Dad!" Sasha yelled, making hi wince.

"Calm down. I see him."

Levi grinned back at him. "You want me to carry you again, or you want the handsome stranger to do it?" he asked.

"Shut up. I can walk." To prove it, Richard opened the truck door and slid down out of the seat, pausing for a moment as a wave of dizziness threatened. It only happened when he moved too fast, and it passed quickly.

Before he could even fully stand, Joey was at his side, trying to get an arm around his waist.

Richard appreciated the nearness of him, but said, "You guys – I can walk. It was my arm I hurt, remember?"

"Yeah," said Levi, "But you're so slow."

Sasha laughed. "Daddy's a turtle."

Richard looked at Joey. "Could you please ward off my tormentors while I go in and hide?"

Joey looked at Sasha and Levi and then stage whispered, "Nah. I think I'm sticking with you. There's something wrong with them."

Sasha wiggled her little body in between the two men. "I'll help, Daddy."

Joey grinned down at her. "You're the boss."

Epilogue

Joey was standing at the newly built corral, one boot on the bottom rung. Steve, standing beside him and watching Sasha ride around the ring, said, "Lemmee get this straight. You're staying here." He pointed toward the ground.

"Yep."

"With him?"

He pointed at Richard, standing on the patio near the grill, talking to Cruz about something. Joey let his eyes linger there for a moment and couldn't help the smile that curled his lips. He'd been thinking long and hard about cutting back on his adventurous life, but then realized that he wasn't cutting back – he was just trading one kind of adventure for another. "Yep."

Steve thought about that. "Is it serious?"

"Yep." Joey took a breath. "I think it is."

"And you're taking six months off work?"

"Yep."

"And you want me to run the operation while you do it."

"Yep."

"Would you stop saying yep?"

Joey grinned. "Yep."

Steve scratched his head. "And would you stop grinning like that? You been doin' it since last week and it's freaky."

It was true. Joey felt like he'd been smiling for days, and it felt good. The job for Levi was finished, the coyotes were back to a smaller, more manageable pack, and his work was done for a while. He could afford to take the time and enjoy this unexpected but welcome turn his life had taken.

Richard came up behind him and slung an arm across his shoulders, making him jump. "Steaks in ten," he said to Steve. "Grab a plate."

Steve looked from Joey to Richard and back to Joey. He looked like he wanted to say something, but then just shook his head and sauntered off.

"He all right with your leave of absence?" Richard asked.

Joey reached down and squeezed his hand. It was the best he could do right now, in front of Sasha, even though he wanted to do more. A lot more.

He wasn't used to having a child around, and he found that intimacy was something that happened after bedtime. They'd had to get pretty damned creative these last few days. Joey considered it a challenge. "He will be, once he thinks about it. Steve doesn't like change all that much, but he'll adjust."

"Good." Richard leaned in and kissed him softly on the lips. "Because I want all of your attention for a while."

Cruz whistled from the patio, making both of them – and everyone else – turn to look. He was wearing a neon orange apron today, and it matched his hat. "You boys come get it while it's hot. Let's get this party started!"

Joey and Richard grinned at each other. "You heard the man," Joey said.

"I'll pry the kid off the horse. You grab the food. Medium and small for her. Medium rare for me, please."

"You got it."

Joey made them plates, but the whole time he kept an eye on Richard and Sasha, who did not want to get off Blueberry and did not want steak and did not want to rest. Richard handled her like a pro, he thought, and then he wondered if he would ever have that kind of relationship with her. Not like a father, but...yeah, maybe like a father. Like Cusp had been with him and Mack.

He carried plates to the picnic table and waited for Richard to come. When they did, he cut up Sasha's steak for her.

"Nice," Richard said, looking. "You've got a way with triangles."

"It's cause I'm an axe predator."

He sat down and Richard squeezed his thigh under the table.

This was the real party, he thought later, watching Richard carry a sleepy Sasha into the house. What he did before, that was just killing time. This was the good stuff, and he was ready and willing to experience every moment of it.

Books by DJ Monroe

BROKEN BLUE BOOK 1
WITH GREAT POWER COMES great responsibility.

Levi King is the most successful horse rancher in the south-eastern United States. He's got it all, but he's also got a lot on his plate - salaries to cover, horses to train, the biggest ranch in the valley - and it's all on him. Everyone around him needs his time and attention, so how did he end up volunteering his ranch for the Wide Open program, an organization designed to give ex-cons a second chance at life? Just what he needs – another responsibility. Even worse, this new responsibility has a cheeky grin, a fine body, and a way of making Levi's blood run hot.

When Cruz Baltimore steps out of the police cruiser and sees the man who's given him a second chance, he's way more than grateful – he's entranced. Levi King is dead serious, wicked sharp, and sizzling hot. Not that he'd be interested in a screw-up like Cruz. Still, Cruz can't help himself. Levi is a strong man, king of his domain. He's a man with a destiny - Cruz just knows he wants to be part of it.

SONS OF GLORY BOOK 1

TWO STRONG WILLED HEROES. Two fiery tempers. Will their hearts go down in flames?

Valor Moretti is not happy to be home. In fact, he swore he'd never set foot in Patriot, Texas again. For years he's traveled around the country as a freelance firearms instructor, happy to be anywhere but Glory Ranch. Now that he's here and his inheritance is on the line, all he has to do is keep his temper and his cousins under control for the next year, and he's home free. He didn't plan on the hot-headed, way-too-sexy Yankee renting the cottage out back, and he definitely didn't plan on the kind of attraction that promised to set his heart on fire.

Kent Massey hates Texas. He hates the heat, he hates that slow drawl accent, and he hates that he's trapped here for at least a month while he trains Patriot's newest K-9 police officer. He especially hates his landlord – that man is a menace. Out shooting handguns at the crack of dawn, making Kent's life miserable, and sticking his nose in where it doesn't belong. It's enough to drive him crazy, especially when he discovers that he'll be working with the guy. His only option is to deal with it, but that doesn't mean he has to like it.

The two men are like fire and ice, oil and water. But when push comes to shove and real danger comes to Glory Ranch, they'll have to set aside their differences and face their true feelings before somebody gets killed.

TWO BEAUTIFUL MEN, one simple mistake, and a
once-in-a-lifetime chance at love.

Lincoln

Lincoln is done. When his lover walks out and leaves him
with a Dear John letter and a broken heart, he knows for a fact
that he will never fall into that trap again. He sucks at love,
and he knows it. If only he could explain that to the busybody
across the hall - the last thing he needs is to witness that guy's
happily ever, the kind that he's lost forever.

Colton

Colton loves playing matchmaker, and he's determined to
make sure his gorgeous neighbor Lincoln finds true love after a
bad breakup. After all, everyone should be as happy as him. But

when his own relationship falls apart, he has to rethink every-thing he thought he knew about love.

The problem is, his neighbor Lincoln makes it hard to think at all.

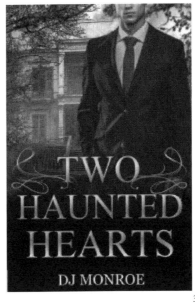

3

A GAY ROMANCE NOVEL about haunting, healing, and timeless love.

Charles Bedford, former author of popular bestselling books, hasn't worked for months. His lover Kyle is dead, and most days Charles doesn't want to be alive either. When he stumbles upon a rambling old plantation home deep in the heart of Virginia, he buys it, figuring it might be just the thing to pull him out of his depression. It's time to move on, and Charles needs a project. He doesn't realize, at first, that he's stepping into an age-old mystery and a second chance at love.

The big mansion is creepy and more than a little lonely, so when a handsome stranger named Stony shows up at his door, telling stories of murder and secrets and forbidden loves from

---

long ago, Charles is more than intrigued – he's downright excited, for the first time in a long while. Maybe Stony can help
him figure out why he constantly feels like he's being watched,
and why one room of the house makes him sick with fear.
Something terrible clearly happened in this crumbling mansion, and Charles hopes that Stony has the ability to heal the
old place - and maybe help him heal his heart, too.

Made in United States
Orlando, FL
25 March 2025

59856417R00109